An Irish Christmas

Escape to Ireland Book 6

Michele Brouder

Chapter One

"Hi, Gram," Jo Mueller called out, bringing in two bags of groceries and setting them down on the kitchen table. Sounds from the television drifted in from the living room as she unloaded everything, put the food away, folded the canvas bags, and tucked them into the broom closet. She filled the kettle and set it on the stove.

She walked through the dining room to the front parlor. Gram was in her recliner, feet up, a crocheted afghan on her lap, her white hair forming a halo around her head. Her cat, Percy, sat on one of the arms of her chair, and she absently petted him, her eyes glued to the television.

Gram was watching *The Quiet Man*. Again. She and Jo knew all the lines. The movie held a special place in Gram's heart, having been a favorite of hers even before she emigrated from Ireland to New York at age eighteen. It reminded her of village life and growing up in rural Ireland.

"Hi, Gram, it's me," Jo said quietly, not wanting to startle her.

Gram broke into a smile. Her blue eyes twinkled. "Hello, Jo. Are you coming from work?" When Jo nodded, she asked, "How was your day?"

Jo shrugged. "Oh, you know, the usual." Jo worked retail, at a clothing store in the shopping mall. The job itself wasn't bad, but her manager was a piece of work. There was no pleasing her.

Her grandmother narrowed her eyes. "Is that boss of yours giving you grief?"

Jo didn't want to worry her, so she kept it vague. "Same thing, different day."

"You should quit that job. They don't value you there. Don't ever stay in a place where you're not appreciated."

That wasn't an option. Not when her roommate had moved out six months earlier, leaving Jo responsible for all the bills.

When Jo didn't respond, Gram said, "You can certainly find another job in the mall, especially with Christmas coming up. You've got experience."

That was true. She'd been working at the mall since high school. But the idea of starting a whole new job search was too much to think about after a long day at work.

"How about a sandwich?" Jo asked.

"If there's salami there, that'll be fine. If not, then whatever you're having."

Jo nodded and headed back to the kitchen. She prepared two salami sandwiches, one for her grandmother and one for herself. They both enjoyed them the same way: with butter on the bread and some mustard. She opened a package of eclairs and put one on a small dessert plate, knowing Gram always liked a sweet with her meal. Once the kettle boiled, she made the tea, and after carrying everything in, she sat down on the sofa across from her grandmother.

"What's new with you?" her grandmother said, lifting half of her sandwich off the plate.

Jo shrugged. "Nothing, really." If her life got any less exciting, it'd probably kill her. It seemed all she did was work, even more so lately since one of the girls had broken her wrist and was out on disability. Jo welcomed the extra hours, though, as they meant a bigger paycheck at the end of the week.

"How's the sketching going?" Gram asked.

"Let me show you," Jo said, perking up. She pulled her sketch pad out of her bag and flipped the pages until she reached her latest piece, a portrait of one of the retirees who came into the food court every day and sat on a bench near the water fountain. She handed it to her grandmother.

Gram studied it. "You've got a lot done since you last showed me."

Jo nodded.

"This is brilliant, Jo. I love the detail of his face and hands. And the way you sketched his shoulders conveys his weariness," Gram said, handing the sketch pad back to her. "Art is your calling. You should go to college for that."

Jo put the pad back in her bag. Most of her friends had already graduated from college a couple of years before. But college wasn't on her horizon. She couldn't add any extra expenses right now. Maybe someday.

"Are you dating anyone?"

Jo laughed. Gram always asked this question. "Nope. Jimmy, the security guard at the mall, is still bugging me to go out with him. He thinks we'd make a great couple."

Her grandmother rolled her eyes. "Jimmy shouldn't think so much, he might get hurt," she said, shaking her head. She'd met him once when Jo had taken her Christmas shopping the previous year. Gram hadn't been impressed. "I'm not quite sold on Jimmy," she'd said at the time.

Jimmy wasn't so bad. He was always stopping into the store where Jo worked to "chat her up," as Gram would say. It could be awkward sometimes, especially when Jo's boss was always lurking, ready to pounce and tell her what she was doing wrong.

"Do you like him?" Gram asked, chewing thoughtfully.

"I like him as a friend."

Gram nodded. "Ah, he's been relegated to the friend zone. I'm not surprised. I can't see there being a lot of passion with Jimmy."

"Gram!"

"Passion is an important part of a relationship," Gram said knowingly.

"He's a good guy," Jo countered.

"I don't doubt that. But is he good enough for you?"

Jo answered tentatively, as if stepping out on ice and wondering if it would support her weight or crack beneath her, causing her to fall in. "He's nice . . ."

Gram shook her head. "That settles it. He's not for you."

Jo burst out laughing, and her grandmother regarded her with a thoughtful expression. "Jo, you are such a lovely girl with so much to offer to the *right* person."

"You're my grandmother, you're supposed to say that!"

Gram waved her off. "Anyway, when I rang you this morning, I told you I wanted to talk to you about something," she said. "And what I want to talk to you about is Ireland."

"All right," Jo said. She loved hearing her grandmother's stories about growing up in Ireland. How she had to milk the cows by hand before she headed off to school, or how Gram's father always drank his tea from a saucer and not a cup. How the house didn't have electricity until 1948, and a bathroom wasn't installed inside until 1955, the year Gram left for New York.

"I haven't been back in twenty years, and I'd like to go one more time before I die," Gram announced.

"Oh," Jo said, not expecting this at all. She didn't want to think about Gram dying. Jo couldn't imagine life without her.

"I'd like to go for a month, and I'd like to go in December."

"This December?" Jo asked. "As in, the December that's less than two months away?"

"Yes, it would have to be. I'm eighty-four years old. What if I'm gone by next year?" Gram asked seriously.

"Don't say that," Jo said, her stomach clenching.

Jo worried about her grandmother traveling over to Ireland. It wasn't just around the corner; it was a long flight, and a month was a long time to be away from home.

"Who will you go with?" Jo asked, thinking Aunt Marie would be the perfect travel companion.

"Why you, of course!" Gram laughed.

"Me? Why me?" Jo asked, unable to hide her surprise.

"Why not you? I'd love to show you where I grew up," Gram said. "Besides, we've always talked about going together."

They'd been talking about it since Jo was eleven, and she'd like to go. She'd like to do a lot of things: go to college, find the love of her life, develop her art. But it all felt like it was some far-off, nebulous dream, when the reality was that bills needed to be paid, and she needed to work her crappy job to pay them.

"I'd love to see Ireland, but two things come to mind," Jo said, squirming in her seat. "First, I couldn't afford a trip like that. And second, I can't take a month off from the store. Especially at Christmas."

Gram scoffed. "This is my treat. I'll pay for it. And as for your job, are you curing cancer over there?"

Jo shook her head. "Well, no, of course not, but—"

"Your boss doesn't deserve you. It would serve her right. Let her scramble around during the holiday season trying to find someone to replace you."

Jo grimaced. "I couldn't let you pay for my share."

"Oh yes you could. I can't take it with me. And when I die, the little bit I have will go to your dad and Marie. You're to get all my jewelry, of course, it's in my will, but let me do this for you now," Gram said. "Besides, we wouldn't have to pay for accommodation. Hasn't Bridie always said that I could stay with her any time?" Bridie Twomey had been Gram's neighbor and best friend growing up.

"But at Christmas?" Jo said. Gram's plan was like a boat with so many holes in the hull that it was rapidly sinking to the bottom of the ocean.

"I'd like to see my homeplace one more time," Gram said wistfully. "At my age, anything can happen, and I don't know if I'll be able enough for it next year."

"Gram, it's lack of income coming in for the month that prevents me from jumping up and down with joy at the prospect," Jo confessed.

"Let me pray to St. Anthony and in the meantime, I'll ring Bridie and see if she's up for some houseguests."

Jo didn't put too much faith in her grandmother's dream to go to Ireland at Christmas. There were so many reasons it couldn't work out, even beyond the not-working part. She could certainly understand her grandmother's desire to go back. She'd always spoken of it with a faraway look in her eyes.

When Jo arrived at her parents' house for dinner the following week, her father greeted her at the door.

Jo unraveled her scarf and brushed off a few snowflakes. It wasn't unusual to see light snow in New York in early November, but they wouldn't see any real accumulation for a few weeks—hopefully, in time for a white Christmas.

"Hi, Dad," Jo said as she hung her coat in the hall closet. She pulled off her hat and put it on the closet shelf. Her hair felt matted to her head, and her cheeks were flushed red with cold. She pulled a tissue from her pocket and wiped her nose.

"What's this I hear your grandmother wants to go to Ireland for Christmas?" her father asked, his hands on his hips.

"Oh yeah, she mentioned that to me when I was over there last week," Jo said, passing her father and heading to the kitchen for a cup of tea. She rubbed her hands together and blew on them.

Upon entering the kitchen, she found her mother at the stove, stirring a pot. Jo leaned over and peered in. "Chili? It's perfect for this weather. How are you, Mom?"

"I'm fine, but your father is stressed out about your grandmother."

Jo shrugged, pulling a spoon out of the drawer. She took a spoonful of chili from the pot and blew on it a couple of times before putting it in her mouth. "*Ow*, that's hot!"

Getting back to her mother's statement, Jo said, "Gram must be feeling homesick. She's stuck in the house too much. I'll take her to the movies and lunch over the weekend."

Her father stood in the doorway. "She's already called Bridie. According to my mother, Bridie is only too delighted to have you *both* stay."

"Oh jeez, I told Gram I couldn't go," Jo explained.

"Your grandmother is home right now, packing her bags," her father said, his face reddening.

Jo bit her lip. Dad had been trying to get Gram to move in with them for the past three years. He worried about his mother endlessly.

Jo started setting the table. The tea could wait until after dinner. A bowl of hot chili was just the thing. As her father rambled on in the background about his mother's travel plans, her mother doled out chili and said nothing. Jo set out a loaf of crusty bread and the butter dish, then rummaged through a drawer for a bread knife.

Her mother finished garnishing each bowl of chili with a dollop of sour cream and some shredded cheddar and carried the bowls to the table. She nodded to Jo, indicating she should sit. Jo's father pulled out his chair, scraping it across the linoleum, and sat down.

"When will Marc be home for Christmas?" Jo asked. Her brother was in Philadelphia, in his first year of residency. He was older than Jo by two years and although they were as opposite as day was from night, they got along well. Always had. He was ambitious and a go-getter and had known he wanted to be a doctor since he was fifteen. Jo, on the other hand, feared she'd be sponging meals off her parents for the rest of her life.

"He'll be home by the twentieth," her mother answered.

"I guess I'll have to be the bad guy and go over there tomorrow and tell my mother she can't go on this trip," Jo's father said.

Jo's mother sighed, and both Jo and her father looked over to her.

"You think I'm wrong, Barbara?" Jo's father asked, raising his voice.

"I understand your concerns, Bill," Jo's mother started. Jo shoveled chili into her mouth without taking her eyes off her parents. "But I think you should let your mother go." She picked up the plate of bread and handed it to her husband. "Bread?"

This is a surprise, thought Jo.

Bill stared at his wife with his mouth hanging open as if she'd just revealed the most incredible thing about herself. "How about the fact that my mother is eighty-four years old and hasn't been to Ireland in over two decades? Not to mention it's a six-hour trip by plane," he countered.

"Your mother has always wanted to go to Ireland one last time. And *because* she is over eighty, now is the time."

"You know," Jo interjected, "according to the last census, 9.7 percent of Americans identify themselves as Irish. That's more than double the entire population of Ireland, which is just under five million people."

Her parents glanced at her and then back at each other.

"That's brilliant, Barbara, just let my mother swan off across the Atlantic Ocean by herself," Bill said, waving his hand in the air, his face getting redder.

Barbara scowled. "Of course not. Don't be ridiculous. Your mother is perfectly capable of visiting Bridie by herself, but obviously she would need someone with her for the flight over and back. Jo can go. It would be perfect for both of them."

Jo's spoon stopped midair. Why did her mother think her accompanying her grandmother would be perfect for her? What was she talking about?

"Um, I don't think I can get the time off work," Jo said.

"Of course you can," her mother said.

"It's not just that," Jo persisted, noticing her father was quiet, trying to process all of this. "I really couldn't afford to take all that time off." As it was, she usually took the pay owed to her for personal time and worked during her vacations.

"We'll figure something out," her mother said.

"It sounds like you've got it all worked out already," Bill said to his wife.

Barbara smiled sweetly. "I have, actually."

Jo wondered if her mother realized how she struggled financially. She must be drinking from the same water source as her grandmother.

CHAPTER TWO

IAN TWOMEY SAT ON his sofa, staring out the front window. It wasn't even five in the evening and it was dark outside. He'd never realized before how much he hated November. He saw the outside light go on at his grandmother's house next door. She'd be bringing around his tea soon.

Right on cue, there was a rap on the front door, followed by the appearance of his grandmother, carrying some foil-wrapped sandwiches. She was a small woman with sharp green eyes and a crown of dyed red hair. At her heels was Scruff, her Yorkshire terrier.

"There you are, Ian," she said with a laugh. "What are you doing sitting in the front window? In the dark no less?" She sailed past him, not really expecting an answer. A moment later, she popped her head out from the kitchen. "Come on, then, I've got some grub for you."

His Nana was from another era. The big dinner was eaten every afternoon while she watched the one o'clock news. Later, in the evening, there was "tea," or what some people called supper.

Ian said nothing, just picked up his crutches and hobbled into the kitchen. He avoided looking down; he didn't want to see his ankle and be reminded of the injury that had ended his career with the Irish Rovers, Ireland's national rugby team.

Nana set a place for him at the table. She removed the dirty plate from his dinner earlier in the day. She went over to the bin by the back door and scraped the remnants into it.

"Nana, you don't have to do that," he said. What did it say about him that he couldn't clean up after himself and that his grandmother had to do it for him?

She straightened up. "I don't mind." For eighty-four, she was pretty spry.

She circled back to the table and removed the tin foil from a plate and set it in front of him. There were two sandwiches: one was ham and coleslaw on white bread, the other was roast chicken, stuffing, and mayo on whole wheat. Cut into quarters.

"You didn't have to go to all this trouble, Nana," he said like he did with every plate she brought up.

"It's no trouble at all," she said with a smile. "Sure, aren't I making a sandwich for myself?"

Ian frowned; Nana was in a better mood than usual if that was even possible. With a glance in her direction, he wondered if she'd been making the Christmas cake and nipping at the sauce.

"Did I tell you that Mary's coming over for a visit?" Nana said, pulling up a chair across the table from Ian.

He had met Mary Mueller, Nana's best friend from childhood, the last time she'd visited. He'd been a young boy then, maybe ten, maybe eleven. When he still had his professional rugby career ahead of him, instead of behind him.

"She'll be here for Christmas," Nana said. "Come on, Ian, eat up. You're wasting away to nothing."

More to please her than to appease any sort of an appetite, Ian picked up one of the sandwiches and took a bite. Chicken and stuffing on bread was pure comfort food, but he was beyond being comforted. He slipped a bit of the sandwich beneath the table to the dog.

"Where's she staying?" he asked. "And how long will she be here?"

"They're staying with me, and they'll be here for a month," Nana said, smiling broadly. "It's wonderful. I've got so much to do before they get here."

"They?" he asked.

"Mary's bringing her granddaughter with her," Nana explained.

Oh terrific, Ian thought. Another pair of gawkers to witness his plight. He'd have to endure their looks of pity or worse, stupid questions. No, thanks. He would remain holed up in his house, as usual.

Bridie paused what she was doing and said, "You know, maybe you could show her around. She's about your age."

"That's probably not a good idea," he said quickly. He wasn't playing tour guide to anyone.

But Nana continued, undaunted. "She won't want to hang around Mary and me, she's too young for that. That'll be perfect."

He didn't bother protesting. What would be the point? His grandmother was going to do what she wanted to do. When the time came, he'd make himself scarce.

And then there was Christmas. Last Christmas, when he still had his career, seemed a lifetime ago. He wondered if he should stay at a hotel until Nana's guests left. The thought of company and the biggest holiday of the year overwhelmed him.

"I might go away for Christmas," he said, although he was supposed to be starting physical therapy. As soon as he returned their phone calls. He didn't know when that would be. He was feeling inert these days.

Nana's face crumpled. "What do you mean? Go away? But you only just got home from rehab!"

He was sorry he'd said anything.

Nana got up and walked over to the sink to fill the kettle. "You can't go away now. I've been looking forward to you coming home for months." She turned her back to him to turn on the electric kettle. Ian took the opportunity to feed the dog another quarter of a sandwich.

With her back still to him, Nana said, "And stop feeding the dog from the table."

Ian sighed, picked up another sandwich, and said to Scruff, "Sorry, buddy."

Nana droned on about how wonderful Christmas was going to be. When he was up in rehab outside of Dublin, she used to call him every few days to encourage him. She'd send him Mass cards from the shrine at Knock or from the Redemptorists in Limerick. She'd never met a candle she didn't light or a prayer she didn't say.

She sat down. "And what's the delay with the physical therapy starting at home?"

"I canceled that appointment," he grumbled.

Nana's mouth fell open. "Why? This is the third time you've canceled. You don't want to be on crutches for the rest of your life, do you?"

Before Ian could answer, there was a knock at the front door, followed by his sister Fiona barging through. In each hand, she carried a canvas bag filled with groceries. She was all smiles.

"Hi, Nana," Fiona said. She held up the bags and said to Ian, "I've brought you some groceries."

Ian sighed. His house was filled with two more people than he wanted.

"How's Grace?" Nana asked Fiona of her partner.

"She's fine, said she'll pick you up this weekend and take you Christmas shopping if you'd like."

"I would, thank you very much," Nana said. When Fiona first announced she had a girlfriend, they'd all worried how Nana would take it. But she'd merely shrugged and said, "Love is love." She and Grace got on well.

Fiona nodded at her brother. "Are you keeping that beard then?"

Ian stroked his beard. He'd started growing it in rehab, and he found he liked it. It suited his new identity as a former professional rugby player. A has-been.

"I'm thinking of it."

Nana shook her head. "I liked your clean-shaven look much better."

"Noted."

As Fiona put lunch meat, cheese, and lettuce into the crisper, Nana said, "Fiona, your brother canceled his therapy appointment again."

Fiona stopped what she was doing, a liter of milk in her hand and the door to the refrigerator wide open. "Ian! Why?"

Ian shrugged, not wanting to admit that he had no interest in doing therapy. What was the point? It wasn't like he'd be able to play rugby again. And as he had no plans to ever leave the house, the crutches were enough.

The kettle clicked off, signaling it had boiled. "Anyone want tea?" Fiona asked.

"Are you staying that long?" Ian asked.

"We'll both have a cup," Nana said, ignoring him.

"Ian," Fiona said in her best older-sister voice. She was one of three older sisters, and they'd been telling Ian what to do for as long as he could remember.

Nana's lips had pressed into a thin line, and she was shaking her head. "What's to be done with you, Ian?"

"Nothing, Nana."

Once Fiona had the groceries put away and the tea made, she sat down with Ian and their grandmother. He was dismayed to see Fiona had made herself a sandwich. That meant she'd be there longer. He was almost tempted to tell her to take the sandwich to go.

"Mum had a call from Donal last night," Fiona started.

Ian rolled his eyes. His mother had texted him about it earlier that day. He'd yet to respond.

This was the purpose of Fiona's visit. She'd been sent on a mission by their parents, who spent their winters in Spain. Donal was one of his teammates and his best friend. Ian did not say anything, because he knew Fiona would have her say with no prompting from him.

"How is he doing?" Nana asked. "We never see him around anymore."

"That's because Ian is not answering his phone or his door."

"Oh, Ian," Nana said, disappointment clear in her voice. She sipped her tea.

"I told Mum to tell Donal not to bother ringing on the phone, to just come over, knock, and walk in. He wants to see you," Fiona said, taking a bite of her sandwich.

Ian seethed. They were trying to run his life. Why couldn't they just leave him alone?

"Okay, little brother, you've got to move on with your life. Yes, what happened is awful. But you're still young, and you can't hide out in your house forever," Fiona said.

Ian felt the hair stand up on the back of his neck. He bit his tongue so as not to respond and say something hurtful.

Nana told Fiona about Mary and her granddaughter coming over.

"Oh, that's wonderful," Fiona said. "How old is the granddaughter?"

"About Ian's age."

"Now, that is interesting," Fiona said.

CHAPTER THREE

"I've worked everything out about Ireland," Gram said as they navigated their way through the mall to do their Christmas shopping.

Jo, sweating under her heavy winter coat with the burden of shopping bags in each hand, stopped in her tracks and stared at her grandmother. "What do you mean?" The subject of the trip hadn't been mentioned since last week, and Jo had assumed her grandmother had decided against it. Although Jo could see her mother's point about how her grandmother should go to the land of her birth given that she wasn't getting any younger, she just couldn't see how she could be the one to accompany her.

"Oh, let's go in here. I've got coupons and I want to get your mother an air fryer," Gram said with a nod toward the store in front of them.

"Mom'd like that, she's been talking about getting one," Jo said.

"I know, I pay attention," Gram said.

Jo followed her grandmother into the store, bumping into people as she went. As she worked retail, bringing her grandmother to the mall hardly felt like a day off.

She waited until they reached the housewares department before she picked up the thread of their conversation.

"What did you mean when you said you had everything worked out about Ireland?" Jo asked, hoping maybe she'd decided to postpone her trip until next year when Jo might have a better chance of going with her.

Gram stood in front of a display of air fryers and turned her attention from them to Jo.

"I've spoken to Bridie, and she said she's got plenty of room for the two of us over Christmas. Now, Jo, I'm going to have Aunt Marie buy our airline tickets online. I will pay for your plane ticket."

"What?" Jo asked, not sure if she'd heard properly. It sounded like the two of them were going to Ireland next month. *She must have missed the part where I said I couldn't possibly go,* Jo thought.

Gram repeated what she'd just said.

"I can't have you do that," Jo protested, hoping it would deter Gram.

"It will be my Christmas gift to you." Gram beamed.

Jo thought her grandmother appeared years younger. It made it harder to tell her—again— she wouldn't be able to go. For whatever reason, her grandmother wasn't getting the message.

"Gram, I can't leave my job in the middle of the Christmas season."

"Of course you can," Gram said, turning her attention back to the display. "Now, this one is a six-point-three quart, but this one is five point seven and it comes with tongs and a recipe book. What do you think?"

"Either one," Jo said. Not only was she hot and tired, but she was also hungry. "As I was saying, Gram, I can't just go away on vacation and not work."

Her grandmother waved her hand in a dismissive gesture and chose the smaller air fryer with the tongs and recipe book.

"Don't worry about that," Gram said. "I spoke to Bridie, and we have it all sorted."

"What do you mean?" Jo asked. As much as she loved her grandmother, she didn't like things about her life being "sorted" by other people. Although that sometimes happened. She was too nice at times.

"Bridie's grandson needs a companion. He's going through a difficult time." Gram paused. "Do you need to get anything here, or will we head to the checkout?"

"Why does he need a companion?" Jo asked. She still had to get some things, but she'd come back. The only thing she wanted to do was get out of there. The store was crowded, and she was tired of getting pushed and shoved and standing in long lines.

As they headed toward the checkout, Gram said, "He's been through an ordeal." Her expression appeared pinched.

"What kind of ordeal?" Jo asked. She eyed the registers, looking for the one with the shortest line. "Recovering from his wife having left him? Getting out of a South American prison?"

Her grandmother giggled. "Oh, Jo, you sure are a hoot."

Jo led them to the last register, took the air fryer from her grandmother, and placed it on the conveyor belt. There was a display of wrapping paper next to the register, and Gram pulled out two rolls. One was white with green wreaths, and the other was a red-and-green plaid.

"Bridie said it was a freak accident. While on holiday in the Maldives, he stepped off a curb the wrong way and shattered his ankle. It's got more pins in it than a tailor's mannequin," Gram explained. She shook her head and made a *tsk, tsk* sound.

"How awful for him."

"Bridie said he's having a hard time adjusting. I guess he used to be a player or something or another."

Jo frowned. "A player, like a ladies' man?" That couldn't be right, could it?

Gram laughed. "No, I mean he plays sports. Professionally. Or did. He doesn't play anymore, of course. He'd need two good ankles for that."

As they progressed through the line, Gram pulled her wallet out of her purse. "He's only recently come home from rehab." She shook her head. "The poor lad. Bridie thought maybe if he had someone closer to his own age to hang around with, it would help pull him out of his funk. He's the proud type, so you wouldn't want to mention anything about being a paid companion."

"But I have no experience with that sort of thing," Jo pointed out. If he really needed help, it might be important to have someone qualified. She couldn't just waltz through his door and announce she was there to keep him company. He'd see right through it. Jo eyed her grandmother, thinking she and her friend Bridie were up to no good.

Gram shrugged, not seeing the problem. "So what? You keep me company, don't you?"

"That's different. You're my grandmother."

"It's not that hard. Just be yourself. You're delightful," Gram said.

Jo laughed. "He might not think I'm so delightful, especially if he's having a hard time."

"Bridie said he's in a rut, and it'll be your job to pull him out of it."

Jo raised her eyebrows and exhaled loudly. "No pressure then."

On the day after Thanksgiving, Jo arrived at work early and headed toward the break room to check out the new schedule. It was going to be posted today, and it would include the holiday schedule. She wanted to make sure she had Christmas Eve off. She'd put in her request with her manager, Linda, back in October, offering to work any other day, weekend, whatever, even open the day after Christmas. She just wanted Christmas Eve off as it was the day they celebrated with her mother's side of the family. Linda had smiled, taken the form with her request, and tucked it in her binder.

The break room was empty. This was the busiest shopping day of the year, and everyone else was already out on the floor. There was the schedule in black and white with red-and-green holly and ivy doodled all over it, hanging on the corkboard with all the other notices no one ever bothered to read.

Her eyes zoomed in on Christmas Eve, and there was her name scheduled for noon to eight, which meant she wouldn't get out until almost nine, when the Christmas Eve gathering at her aunt's house would be just about over. Jo pressed her lips together. She was also scheduled to come in the day after Christmas at eight in the morning, and she'd been scheduled for every weekend in December. She studied the rest of the schedule. Colleagues who started after her had either the day before or the day after Christmas off. Her nostrils flared as she exhaled.

Things like this happened because Jo allowed it. She let people walk all over her. Something her grandmother had said came to mind, about not staying in a place where you weren't appreciated. She bit her lip and thought about her options. Would she rather continue to work this crappy job or take the trip of a lifetime with her grandmother? She could put in some applications before leaving for Ireland and maybe even line up an interview or two, all with the caveat that she couldn't begin any new job until January.

The door to the break room opened and her boss appeared.

"Do you think you'll join us out on the floor?" Linda asked.

Even though her chest felt like lead and her voice shook, Jo said, "Linda, I see you've got me scheduled for Christmas Eve. I asked for it off."

"We'd all like to be off for Christmas," Linda said. "See if someone will switch with you."

Jo snorted. Like anyone would switch with her at this time of year.

Linda shrugged. "Oh well. Come on, let's get to work. It's the busiest day of the year."

Usually, it would have ended at that. Jo would have stayed quiet and gotten to work. But not today. She drew in a deep breath.

"Wait a minute, Linda," Jo said.

Linda stopped and said, "I'm not making any changes to the schedule, Jo."

"I know," Jo said. "That's why I'm giving you my two weeks' notice."

Linda stood there, gape-jawed, and Jo sailed past her, heading to work. She felt lighter than she had in years. For now, she

decided not to think about the implications of being unem-
ployed.

⎯⎯⎯ℓℓℓ⎯⎯⎯

It was raining in Dublin when Jo and Gram arrived early in the
morning on December tenth.

Gram took one look out the window and declared, "It's
always good to come home!" Jo yawned. In the flight over the
Atlantic and with the time change, they had lost six hours,
hours that should have been spent sleeping. It was as if being
back in Ireland took years off her grandmother; she seemed in
better shape than Jo felt. And Gram had sixty years on her.

They collected their luggage and went outside to the taxi
stand. Bridie had assured them there was no need to get a rental
car as she had a car and would do any driving. But Gram had
decided to splurge on a taxi to save Bridie the two-hour drive
to pick them up at the airport.

To Jo's great relief, she'd managed to secure a new job before
they left. It was at a coffee shop near her home, so she'd be able
to walk to work and save on gas, and she would start the day
after they got home from their trip. They weren't due to return
to the US until the seventh of January. Gram had said she
wanted to be in Ireland for January sixth, or what in Ireland
was referred to as Little Christmas or the Women's Christmas.
Jo was excited to see what that was all about. All Gram had said
was that it was for the women.

By the time their cab reached the motorway, Gram was
leaning against Jo, dozing off in the back seat. As she slept, Jo
watched, fascinated, as the scenery passed by. Despite the bleak
weather and the gray skies, the countryside was beautiful. She
couldn't believe how green everything was, even in December.

In some places—maybe it was due to the dark sky—the grass almost looked blue. Endless vales and pastures stretched to the horizon. They passed hills and valleys and cows and stone ruins, and she couldn't wait to capture it all with the new pencils and sketch pads she'd bought for the vacation. She loved it already, and because Gram had been born here, it felt even more special.

When Gram awoke, she straightened up and asked, "Are we almost there?"

"Almost," Jo said, returning her attention to the scenery. "Does it ever snow here?"

"Sometimes, but not as much as it used to," Gram replied. "The east coast, where we're going, and the north would get more snow than the west. The gulf stream keeps the temperatures on the west coast moderate and not cold enough for snow. When I was a young girl, we'd get some serious snow at home."

"I hope we get snow for Christmas," Jo said thoughtfully. "Are you excited about visiting your homeplace?"

Gram's smile was wide. "Oh, I am. It's a pity that no one has lived in it for more than thirty years."

Jo nodded sympathetically. Gram's brother had inherited the home and the farm but died young, without any family. The property had then passed onto Gram, who was well settled by this point in the States. At the time, they couldn't afford to keep it, and it was sold. The land continued to be used for cattle grazing, but the house fell to ruin—a bitter regret for Gram.

They were quiet until they pulled into the little village in County Wexford where Bridie lived.

Gram sat forward and nodded out the window. "See that boarded-up building there? That used to be Hogan's Dance

Hall. Bridie and I had a lot of fun there." She appeared wistful. "If I had a penny for every dance I danced there . . ." After a bit, she said, "And didn't I meet your grandfather at a dance in New York?"

Jo knew the story of how Granddad had crossed a crowded room and asked Gram to dance. They'd danced all night. Granddad used to say he'd never seen anyone prettier than Gram.

The cab driver slowed in front of a long peach-colored bungalow. In the front window stood a Christmas tree, its multicolored lights twinkling. At the side of the house, a footpath led around back to a newer-build bungalow with a stone front. Jo wondered if this was the home of Bridie's grandson.

The cab driver parked and jumped out to open the trunk. As Jo helped Gram out of the back seat, the front door of the house opened, and a diminutive figure appeared in the doorway. She smiled and waved to them, walking down the footpath toward them. Her short hair was dyed red, and Jo figured she couldn't be more than five feet tall.

Gram hurried toward her friend with Jo in tow. The cab driver brought up the rear, carrying their luggage.

Bridie embraced Gram and gushed, "You are so very welcome!"

The two elderly women held on to each other for a while and when they pulled apart, Gram introduced Jo to Bridie.

"Welcome, Jo. I appreciate you bringing your grandmother all this way to see me," Bridie enthused. "Oh, Mary, she's the image of you when you were young."

"Isn't she?"

"Well, let's not stand out here in the damp, you must be exhausted," Bridie said, waving them inside.

Jo followed Gram inside the house. As soon as she crossed the threshold, she was blasted with warmth. She was getting tired and when she got tired, she got cold, so the heat was welcome. The narrow hallway was carpeted and wallpapered in shades of cream and scarlet. A quick peek in through the sitting-room door to the right revealed two paintings above the mantel: one of the Sacred Heart of Jesus, the other of Elvis Presley. Jo smiled; her grandmother was a big fan of the King of Rock 'n' Roll too.

At the entrance to the kitchen stood the littlest dog Jo had ever seen. He wagged his tail.

"And that's Scruff," Bridie said.

"He's so cute," Jo said, bending down to pet him. The dog wagged his tail faster.

If Jo had thought the house was warm, the kitchen was even warmer. A big cream-colored range stood to one side. Bridie threw in a piece of wood to keep it going.

"Don't know what I'd do without that," she said. To Gram and Jo, she said, "You must be so tired. Why don't you have something to eat, and then you can have a lie-down for a few hours."

Both Gram and Jo nodded, each starting to wilt with the aftereffects of jet lag. Bridie indicated that they should take a seat at her kitchen table, where two place settings were already laid out. Just looking at them made Jo's stomach growl.

As Bridie cooked something on the stove, she and Gram caught up on local gossip. Jo said nothing, just listened. It was amazing how they could pick up where they'd left off. It was as if they'd seen each other last week instead of twenty years ago.

Jo could feel herself beginning to nod off, but when Bridie set down two plates of fried eggs, beans, sausages, and rashers in front of them, she immediately perked up. The dog appeared beside her chair.

"Scruff, go lie down," Bridie said firmly, and the dog went over to his bed by the stove and collapsed on it with a sigh.

"Looks good!" Jo pronounced, picking up her fork and digging in.

Bridie laughed. "I like to see someone with a good appetite."

"I don't know where she puts it!" Gram said.

"You used to be like that, Mary," Bridie said. "Remember? You always ate what I didn't finish. My father used to say you had a hollow leg."

"I do like my food," Gram said with a smile.

Bridie put a plate of toast in the middle of the table.

"We're foodies, right, Gram?" Jo asked with a gentle nudge.

Gram laughed. "I guess we are."

Bridie poured tea into mugs. She put the sugar bowl and a creamer of milk in the middle of the table. "Would you like orange marmalade or black currant jam?"

"Orange marmalade," Jo and Gram said together.

Bridie fixed herself a cup of tea and helped herself to a slice of toast, which she covered with butter and marmalade.

"How's Ian doing?" Gram asked.

Bridie sighed. "Not well at all. Physically, he'll heal but mentally, he isn't in a good place." She shook her head and her eyes grew wet. "His career with the Irish Rovers is finished, and he's very bitter about it."

"That's understandable, a young lad like that with a brilliant career," Gram sympathized.

Jo's ears perked up at the mention of Ian. She supposed if she was going to be his companion, she'd better learn as much as she could about him. She cut up a sausage and forked a piece into her mouth.

"What's ironic is how he took such a beating on the field during his career, and yet one wrong step did so much damage," Bridie said.

"That's awful. It sounds like a freak accident," Gram said. "What about his girlfriend?"

Jo spread marmalade on a piece of toast and redirected her attention to Bridie. She was still turning over in her head the fact that Ian had a girlfriend. Where was she in all of this? Certainly, he wouldn't want Jo hanging around if there was a girlfriend on the scene. How awful would that be?

Bridie's expression was one of distaste. "As soon as it was clear his career was over, she broke up with him."

Jo could see that the girl had scored herself no points with Ian's grandmother. She couldn't blame Bridie. It was low to dump someone just because of a career-ending injury.

"He was taken into surgery at a hospital in the Maldives, but it didn't heal right. He had to have a second operation when he came home, but his ankle will never be right again," she said.

Gram sighed. "That's a lot for a young man to have to deal with."

"He's struggling. He only just got out of rehab a few weeks ago." Bridie picked up the stainless-steel teapot and refilled their cups. Jo helped herself to another piece of toast, buttering it up and putting more marmalade on it. Listening to Ian's tale of woe had removed any feelings of jet lag.

"He's angry," Bridie finally said. She stared out the window. "He's not the Ian I knew. That we all knew."

"Maybe he just needs time," Gram said.

"I suppose he does, but he doesn't come out of his house, and he doesn't go anywhere," Bridie said.

"Does he get physical therapy at home?" Jo asked.

"He's been referred, but he keeps canceling the appointment."

Jo winced. "That's too bad."

"But that's where I'm hoping you will help," Bridie said, smiling.

When Gram first mentioned the companion position, even though Jo had been skeptical, she thought it might alleviate her worries over income while she was away, especially since she'd gone and quit her job. But now, hearing about Ian, she wasn't so sure. It sounded like he had a lot to deal with and sitting around and making small talk might not fit the bill.

Bridie said, "I know this won't be easy. And you certainly didn't expect to come over to Ireland to sit with someone who is refusing all help."

That was it in a nutshell, Jo thought.

"But he needs to be pulled back to the land of the living. And no matter what I or his parents or his sisters do, it doesn't seem to be working."

"Okay," Jo said, not feeling at all optimistic about her chances if his own family—who loved him and vice versa—could not reach him. She was no miracle worker. Just an average girl who liked to draw. What qualifications did she have to help someone who was going through a traumatic time? None whatsoever. How had she let Gram and Bridie rope her into this? Suddenly, she wanted to go home and forget the whole thing.

"What do you want Jo to do?" Gram asked.

"We're going to have to tread carefully here," Bridie said. "I don't want him to know you're being paid."

Jo grimaced. This wasn't a good idea. "If I'm just keeping him company, I don't need to be paid." How could she take money from someone's suffering?

"No, Jo, a deal's a deal," Bridie said. "I insist on it."

Jo went to protest, but Gram reached out, patted Jo's hand, and gave her a reassuring smile.

"How are you going to get around that, Bridie?" Gram asked. "The part about not telling Ian that Jo's being paid?"

Jo wondered this herself. She couldn't force herself on the man. He had enough to deal with without having the stress of an uninvited guest.

She voiced her concern. "I feel like I'm being foisted on him." She wanted to add "against his will," but refrained.

"Not at all," Bridie said with a dismissive wave of her hand. "Eventually, he'll see that it has done him a lot of good."

Jo didn't want to remind Bridie that she was only there for a month. It was a lot of pressure. Her stomach began to tie itself in knots.

"I'll tell him straight away that you're going to keep him company while you're here," Bridie said. "That you don't want to hang around people our age. It'll be a bonus if you can get him out of the house. Sightseeing or something."

Somehow Jo doubted that Ian would want to go sightseeing.

"How does he get around? Does he drive?" Jo asked, unsure, realizing her knowledge of rehab patients and their lives was absolutely zero.

"He's using crutches until his ankle gets stronger. But lately, he seems to be spending more and more time just sitting around and staring. It's as if he's given up. He has a car, but he can't drive it yet."

Next to her, Gram yawned.

"We'll talk about this later," Bridie said. "The two of you need to take a nap."

"We can help with the cleanup," Jo offered.

"Nonsense, that'll take me five minutes," Bridie said. She stood up from the table. "Come on, I'll show you to your room. I hope you don't mind sharing. My other spare room is filled to the rafters."

"We don't mind," Gram said, "do we, Jo?"

Jo shook her head and yawned.

They followed Bridie down another narrow hall. It, too, was wallpapered and carpeted, with family photos and some religious pictures hanging on the wall. Bridie showed them where the bathroom was, then opened the door to their room at the end of the hall, a bright but cozy room with yellow duvets on the twin beds and a big window that overlooked the front lawn and garden and the street beyond.

Jo couldn't wait to collapse on the bed. She made two trips to the front door to carry their luggage back to the bedroom. Gram used the bathroom first and then came back into the room.

"I'll call you in a couple of hours," Bridie said. "You don't want to sleep the whole day, or else you won't sleep tonight."

That sounded good to Jo. She hadn't really thought about what she'd like to do here in Ireland. The usual sights, she supposed. A guidebook would have been helpful. She probably should have picked one up before she left the States. She felt ill-prepared.

Once Bridie left, Jo used the bathroom to wash her face and brush her teeth. When she returned, Gram was already on one of the beds.

"I hope you don't mind, Jo, I took this bed because it's closer to the door and the bathroom," Gram said. Her voice sounded drowsy.

"Not at all, Gram," Jo said. She collapsed on her bed and stared at the ceiling, yawning. "I'm beat."

There was no answer from Gram, and Jo looked over to see she was already sleeping.

Jo was tired and she should have fallen asleep, but she ended up staring at the ceiling for the next few hours, worrying about her role as Ian's companion. Especially the part where he wasn't going to know she was being paid to do it.

The whole thing didn't sound like much fun. Especially for Ian.

CHAPTER FOUR

THROUGH HIS FRONT WINDOW, Ian watched as Nana left her house and made her way up the footpath to his. Earlier that morning, he'd seen the cab pull up in front of her house. Two passengers had gotten out of the back seat, and he vaguely recognized Mary, although he hadn't seen her since he was a kid. The younger of the two women was small in height and even in the dull light of December, he could see that her hair was an auburn shade. *That must be her granddaughter*, he'd thought.

"Oh good, you're up and dressed," Bridie said, coming through the front door.

The day before, he hadn't bothered getting out of bed at all. He'd thought about doing the same today, but the idea of company coming in and standing in his bedroom staring at him in the bed was a bit much even for him.

"I'll be bringing Mary and Jo up later to meet you."

"Hmmm," he said.

"Mary looks the same; she hasn't aged one bit since I last saw her." Nana smiled. "I can't believe I haven't seen her in twenty years. Where has the time gone?"

Ian had no answer for that. Or anything else, for that matter.

"I think it might be nice if you and Jo spent some time together," Nana said casually.

"What? Why?" Ian asked, alarmed. He didn't want anyone up here with him; he wanted to be left alone.

Nana laughed. "I'm sure a young woman would rather spend time with someone her own age rather than Mary and me. She doesn't want to hang around us. We'll be going to bingo and visiting friends. I'm sure she would find that quite boring."

"Have you asked her?" Ian said, disturbed at the direction the conversation was going. He didn't want company. He didn't know this Jo, or whoever she was. What was he supposed to do with her? And did she really come to Ireland to spend her holiday holed up with him, someone who didn't want to leave his house? He highly doubted it.

"I don't need to ask her," Nana said, surprised that he'd even consider this.

That was Nana for you, he thought wryly. She liked to direct everyone's lives to her satisfaction.

"Nana, I really don't want to see anyone," he said firmly.

She waved him away. "Nonsense. You only think you don't want to see people."

Man, she has an answer for everything, he thought.

"It isn't necessary," Ian said with an air of finality he hoped his grandmother would pick up on.

She didn't. "All the same," she said with a sigh, "I'm asking you as a favor."

It was his turn to sigh. This was one thing he could not say no to, for two reasons. First, for as long as he could remember, she'd been a constant, primary, loving force in his life. And second, she'd never asked him for a favor before. She'd never asked him for anything.

He knew he wasn't going to say no. But he thought he'd give it one final try. "Nana, you know I'm not much company these days, so would it be fair to do that to the poor girl?"

Nana waved him off with a laugh. "No worries there. She's a lovely, sociable girl, Ian."

Ian suspected "sociable" might be Nana's way of saying "chatty." That was worse, and it was the last thing he wanted. Someone who talked incessantly. About nonsense. That might be enough to push him over the edge.

Nana stood up, indicating to him that the conversation was over. He eyed his grandmother. For a little woman, she sure was a force to be reckoned with.

Later that afternoon, Ian spied his grandmother with Mary and her granddaughter coming up the footpath toward his house. He groaned. He did not want to meet them. He felt on display. Nana was talking and laughing with Mary, who was next to her. Mary seemed to be holding her own with the chat. Following them was Mary's granddaughter.

Just as Nana had promised, she arrived on Ian's doorstep with her company. There was a knock on the front door, and she and her friends entered. Ian was on the sofa in the middle of his sitting room, out in the wide open, with his crutches propped next to him.

He gritted his teeth, determined to get through the ordeal.

Nana and Mary came at him first.

"Ian, do you remember me? Mary Mueller? I remember you. When I was last here, you were about ten, and you were going through a Nutella phase."

He smiled politely. He did remember that. He'd put Nutella on everything, and his mother had worried that he would end up deficient in vitamins and minerals.

Nana and Mary stood in front of him, talking to him. The girl who had come with Mary hung back. He couldn't see her, and he wondered if she was shy. Or maybe she thought this was just as ridiculous as he did.

Finally, Nana and Mary stepped apart and the girl stepped forward. Her auburn hair tumbled down around her face as she pulled off her hat. She met his gaze and extended her hand. "Hi, I'm Jo."

"Ian." He shook her hand and studied her. Jo Mueller looked to be in her mid-twenties. She was petite and pretty, there was no doubt about that. The color of her hair was amazing.

She nodded toward his crutches. "Your grandmother said you'd been hurt."

That was the polite way of saying he'd been unable to manage one step off the curb. "Yes."

She nodded. "What was rehab like?"

Her question caught him off guard. People tended to avoid him, not knowing what to say or not wanting to come face to face with a washed-up rugby player. Her frankness surprised him.

"It was intense."

Jo raised her eyebrows. "I can't imagine."

She hadn't said "I *can* imagine," because she really couldn't. He was appreciative of that.

It surprised him that she didn't seem embarrassed on his behalf or even shy. What he had noticed was that her warm hazel eyes were clear and bright. It occurred to him that if he had met her before the accident, he'd have thought about asking her out. And now he was supposed to spend time with her? Entertain her while Nana and Mary went off doing who knew what? Why couldn't she have been an older woman with grandchildren or something? Why did she have to be young and pretty? His face reddened.

"This is my first time in Ireland," Jo said.

Nana and Mary went off to the kitchen to make tea for everyone.

Jo headed toward the bookcases that flanked the fireplace. The shelves were crammed with trophies, championship cups, medals, and framed photos of his career.

"Wow, are these all yours?" she asked, her eyes wide. She leaned in to read them.

He was about to say something smart like "No, they belong to the guy next door," but he didn't have the energy for sarcasm, so he simply said, "Yes."

"They're impressive."

The Irish Rovers had had some great seasons, lots of championships, and he'd been a part of that. Past tense.

Jo removed her coat, sat in one of the chairs next to the sofa, and crossed her legs. They were nice and shapely with narrow ankles.

"It really is a beautiful country," she prattled on. "Gram told me so much about it growing up, so it's a thrill to finally be able to see it firsthand. And to be here at Christmastime makes it extra special, especially since my parents and brother will fly over to spend Christmas with us. Christmas is a family holiday, after all."

Ian winced. He hoped her chattiness was due to nervousness and not a personality trait. That would be unbearable. He stared at her, willing her to stop talking.

It failed.

"I suppose with you living here, you take all this beautiful scenery for granted. You're used to it. It's that way back home. We have all these tourist attractions around us, but do we ever go? No, we don't. Only when out-of-towners come to visit us, then we take them on the nickel tour. Do you find it that way here?" she asked.

He shrugged but said nothing.

She gave him a small smile and a nod. She stopped talking, and Ian couldn't help but wonder if she was gearing up for the next round or taking a break to catch her breath. What was taking Nana so long to make the tea?

"Bridie told me you used to play soccer," Jo said.

"Rugby," he corrected.

"He speaks!" she teased with a grin. A pair of dimples bracketed her smile.

When he didn't say anything, she rambled on. "To be honest, I don't know the difference between rugby and soccer."

Ian frowned. How could you confuse rugby with soccer? She must be as thick as a plank.

"And forget about hurling," she said with a giggle. "That sport makes absolutely no sense to me."

Ian scowled at her. What was she on about?

She must have read his expression, because she turned away and muttered, "Alrighty then."

Nana and Gram came through the door with tea. Ian had never been so happy to see anyone in his whole life.

Nana handed a mug of tea to Jo and then to Ian. If it weren't so steaming hot, he would have gulped down the entire contents and then excused himself. He'd had enough.

Mary handed around dessert plates with slices of apple tart and a dollop of cream. Why was it that every time tea was served, a slice of tart or cake had to accompany it? He wolfed down the tart to move things along, namely getting Nana and her guests out of his house.

"Goodness, Ian, slow down, there's more in the kitchen." Nana laughed. "You'd think you never had apple tart before."

"It's nice to see a young man with an appetite," Mary said, winking at him and smiling.

They were all so *cheery*. If they stayed for long, he was sure to die from an overdose of happy. Who were these people? So agreeable. So annoying. So in his space. They were on holiday; didn't they have sights to see? A Blarney Stone to kiss? Irish coffee to drink?

Jo didn't say anything while she ate her tart and took sips of her tea.

"Jo, are there any things you'd like to see while you're here in Ireland?" Nana asked.

"Gosh, I wouldn't know where to begin," Jo gushed. "I do want to do some sightseeing, but I also just want to see how normal Irish people live and how they celebrate Christmas. People such as yourself."

Nana laughed while Ian practically snorted at the term "normal Irish people." What was she expecting? Leprechauns and rainbows?

"Well, you'll get plenty of that," Nana said. "Although I don't know about the normal part." Nana and Mary broke into giggles.

"Ian, Jo's an artist," Nana volunteered.

Jo rushed to speak. "Oh, no, I'm not trained or anything. I just like to sketch and paint."

Ian frowned.

"There's plenty to sketch here in Ireland," Nana said. "Ian, you should take Jo around so she can do some drawing."

"Or maybe she could go with you and Mary," Ian said quickly. Time to torpedo that boat.

Nana shook her head. "Oh goodness, no. What's she going to do? Draw us marking off our bingo cards? I don't think so."

Ian didn't protest fast enough, for Nana announced, "There, that's all settled, you can show her the Irish sights. Have you brought your sketch pad with you, Jo?"

Jo nodded, smiling.

"Good. Tomorrow, first thing."

"And how would I do that?" Ian asked. "I can't drive."

"No worries, we can hire a wheelchair van," Nana said.

Ian saw red and blurted, "I am not going into a wheelchair van! I'm not even in a wheelchair!"

"Then we'll hire a taxi," she said.

"No," he said through gritted teeth.

Nana, Mary, and Jo stared at him, saying nothing.

It was Jo who spoke up first. "Ian doesn't have to show me any sights. I can get around myself. I'm sure there's public transportation."

"Nonsense," Nana said. "We'll work something out." She eyed Ian before turning toward Jo. "Jo, do you drive?"

Jo nodded.

"Perfect. You can drive Ian's car then."

Fortunately, they didn't stay long after that. But as they left, Nana said, "You know what, Ian? Jo can come up later and help you get your decorations up. It'll give the place a bit of cheer, which is so desperately needed."

"Not necessary," he said.

But Nana ignored him, intent on imposing her will. "Jo will be here after seven. I'll have her bring your tea up as well."

Once the door closed behind them, Ian closed his eyes and breathed a sigh of relief.

Why couldn't people just leave him alone?

Chapter Five

After her first meeting with Ian Twomey, Jo was doubtful of Bridie's plan for her to be his companion. If moods were a weather front, he'd be an Arctic one. It was obvious he didn't want to be bothered. He could barely hide his reluctance in taking her around Ireland. She supposed she couldn't blame him. He was dealing with a life-changing injury, and probably the last thing he wanted to do was act as an honorary member of the tourist board. She sympathized; if she had lost the ability to draw, she'd be feeling pretty low herself.

Bridie put down a supper of thick, hearty vegetable soup and brown bread with butter. She spoke about some holiday decorations she'd picked up for Ian that Jo could take up later.

"I get the impression that Ian doesn't want me around," Jo said.

Bridie was quick with a reply. "Ian is confused. He doesn't know what he wants. We need to help him find his way back."

Jo did not miss how she used the word "we." Again, she felt as if she were being corralled. "How are you on a ladder?" Bridie asked.

Jo was trying to keep up with the sudden turn in the conversation. "In a pinch, sure." She was beginning to suspect that Bridie and Gram had been quite a combination when they were younger. It was amazing they'd managed to stay out of trouble. Or jail.

"Perfect!" Bridie announced. "Ian's Christmas lights need to be hung outside."

"I don't know about that," Jo said. She'd never hung lights before and hadn't a clue as to how it might be done.

Bridie gave a dismissive wave. "You'll be grand."

It might be odd to march into someone else's house and start decorating for Christmas, Jo thought. She narrowed her eyes at the two older women, wondering what planet they were on that they didn't see how awkward this might be. Jo concluded that Bridie must really love her grandson to go to all this trouble.

"He's got a tree somewhere, but I don't know where he stores it. You'll have to ask him," Bridie said.

At least decorating would give her something to do. If she was standing around idle, she would get nervous and start talking just to fill the blank spaces. But there was a bigger problem Jo hadn't even considered before she'd arrived.

She found Ian incredibly attractive. Jo hadn't known what to expect, but Ian Twomey wasn't it. Despite his shattered ankle, she could see that he was still a formidable man, all rock-hard muscles and bulging biceps. He wore his dark hair short, and she found the beard intriguing. It lent him an air of ruggedness that she would have liked to investigate further. How would it feel beneath her fingers? How would it feel against her chin if she were to kiss him? No, this was never going to work.

But there was no time to be thinking about how handsome he was. Not only did she live too far away, but he hardly seemed in the mood for a dalliance. Once they finished their soup, Bridie and Gram got ready for bingo up at the complex in town. Realizing she couldn't put it off any longer, Jo gathered her things and made her way up to Ian's house.

It turned out that Bridie had three big boxes of decorations for Ian's house, which Jo somehow managed by herself. The boxes were heavy, and she had to carry them up the footpath one at a time. By the time she set the second box down in front of Ian's door, it had started to rain. She stacked the boxes on top of one another outside the door, and on the top she placed a covered bowl of soup and plate of brown bread for Ian's supper. She knocked on the door. There was no answer. The rain began to come down heavier. She knocked again, this time a little harder. Rain began to lash down, and she pushed the boxes up against the wall so they wouldn't get too wet. When there was still no answer, she knocked and tried the door handle. It was open.

Stepping inside, she called out, "Ian?" She thought she heard music coming from the kitchen.

Jo left the door open and pulled the boxes in one by one. She closed the door and removed her coat, laying it on top of one of the boxes.

"Ian?" she called out again. She headed toward the kitchen, knocked on that door, and gently opened it.

Ian looked up from the table, where he was reading the newspaper. Music emitted from a Bluetooth speaker on the countertop. He was scowling but said nothing. Jo ignored the stormy look in his eyes and focused on his beard. She'd never dated anyone with a beard or a mustache.

"Um, hi," she said. She held up the wrapped bowl and plate. "I've got your supper for you." When he didn't say anything, she set them down on the end of the counter.

"I've brought some Christmas decorations up from your grandmother's house."

"No."

"I'm sorry?" Jo asked, not sure what he meant.

"I mean it's not necessary for you to put up my Christmas decorations," he said, keeping his eyes on the sports section.

"You prefer to do it yourself?" Jo asked, beginning to back out of the room. "That's understandable. I get that. It's your house."

Ian sighed, stopped reading the paper, and looked up, staring at the wall. He still did not make eye contact with Jo.

"No, I just don't plan on putting up any decorations this year," he said. He turned his attention back to the newspaper.

"I see," Jo said. "I kind of understand. You're going through a difficult time, and you don't want holiday cheer forced on you."

Ian stared at her. "Well, thanks, Oprah, for your enlightening insight."

Jo felt her neck get hot. Her intention hadn't been to upset him. But Gram always said the path to hell was paved with good intentions.

She turned around and made to exit. "I didn't mean to offend you. I'll leave," she said firmly.

Jo thought about what she would say to Bridie. She hated being caught in the middle between Ian and his grandmother. This was turning into the hardest job she had ever worked. She had just reached the front door when Ian called out.

"Jo!"

She returned to the kitchen and popped her head in. "Yeah?"

"Put the decorations up, but please leave me out of it."

"All right. Um, one question. Do you have a ladder? Oh, and where is your Christmas tree?" she asked.

Ian frowned. "That's two questions more than I want to answer."

"Could you humor me?" Jo asked. She tried a smile, which resulted in a put-upon sigh from him.

"They're both in the garage. There's a door at the end of the hall that leads to the garage, so you don't have to go outside."

"All right, thanks."

"What is Jo short for?" Ian asked. "Josephine? Joan?"

"No, my full name is Johanna."

"Okay, Johanna," he said. He reminded her, "Don't bother me with anything."

Jo figured she could do this, get his decorations up without troubling him further. She pulled the boxes into the living room and opened them, searching for the lights. If it stopped raining before it got too dark, she would put them up outside. Otherwise, they would have to wait until morning.

The artificial Christmas tree was up on a high shelf in the garage. She spied an aluminum ladder set against a wall, leaned it against the shelves, and climbed it, the rungs rattling noisily beneath her.

As she was stepping down, she took a misstep, but was able to hop off the ladder before falling. But when she did, she knocked over a lawn chair. She landed on top of it, banging her hip. It took her a moment to get her bearings. She stood up and brushed herself off, wincing.

The door to the garage opened and Ian appeared, leaning on his crutches.

"Everything all right?"

"Oh yeah, no problem," she replied, rubbing her sore hip.

Ian nodded, turned, and pulled the door closed behind him.

Jo carted everything into Ian's sitting room. She didn't dare go into the kitchen, respecting Ian's desire to be left alone. She was about to place decorations on the bookshelves next to his trophies when she noticed they were loaded with dust. She'd spied cleaning agents out in the garage on a shelf above the washing machine and dryer, and it only took a few seconds before she located a bag of dustcloths and other usable rags. She gave Ian's sitting room a good dusting and took the vacuum from the garage to give the room a quick vacuuming.

Two hours later, the tree was up and decorated. The rain hadn't let up, so she'd put off exterior illumination for the time being. She was placing some final ornaments on the tree when the front door opened and a young woman came in.

"Hello," said the woman. Jo figured her to be Ian's sister, because the familial resemblance was strong. Like Ian, she was tall, and had the same dark hair and blue eyes. Jo wondered if she was athletic like her brother. Jo herself had two left feet and although she'd tried out for sports in high school, she'd more often than not been relegated to the position of benchwarmer.

Jo put down the ornament she was holding and stepped forward, extending her hand. "Hi, I'm Jo. My grandmother and I are staying with Bridie."

The other woman clasped her hand and broke into a warm smile. "Oh, right. Nana has been so excited about you guys coming over. She's like a kid on Christmas morning."

Jo laughed. "We're just as excited to be here."

"I'm Fiona, by the way." She glanced around the sitting room. "I see Nana has roped you into one of her ideas."

"I don't mind. I love Christmas."

"It looks great. Hopefully, it'll cheer him up a bit. How is he today?"

Jo had nothing to compare Ian's mood with, so she said, "I don't know. I'm staying out of his way."

The smile on Fiona's face disappeared. "Don't let him push you around. He was the youngest in our family and the only boy after three girls, so he was a bit spoiled. But don't be afraid to keep him in line."

"Okay," Jo said. Somehow, she couldn't imagine ordering Ian around, but she nodded, trying to be a good sport.

"Time to go into the lion's den!" Fiona laughed. She waved goodbye to Jo and disappeared into the kitchen.

CHAPTER SIX

Ian looked up as Fiona sailed through the kitchen door. He'd finally gotten around to reheating the supper Nana had sent over and was just finishing it. He'd not seen Jo since that incident in the garage. She hadn't said, but he thought she might have fallen. He was glad she hadn't hurt herself. He only had one pair of crutches. After that, he'd put in his earbuds so he wouldn't hear anything and be tempted to investigate.

As promised, she had stayed out of his way. And she had left him alone. He only hoped she hadn't gone overboard with the Christmas decorations. He didn't want to stroll into his sitting room and find he was in the middle of a winter wonderland.

"What's the news, Fiona? How's Grace?" Ian asked.

"She's fine, busy preparing a legal brief, so she's working late tonight," Fiona said. She removed her coat and hung it on the back of a chair.

"How are you today?" she asked.

"The same as yesterday," Ian replied.

"That good, huh?" Fiona teased.

Even Ian had to smile.

"I just met Jo. She's done a great job decorating. It looks really Christmassy."

Ian grimaced. "That's what I'm afraid of."

Fiona laughed. She put the kettle under the tap and filled it and turned it on. "So what has Nana strong-armed Jo into doing?"

Ian shrugged. "I have no idea. Keeping me company, I guess. I'm sure Jo really wanted to come to Ireland to put up Christmas decorations."

"Why don't you take her around? Show her some sights?" Fiona suggested casually, staring out the window over the kitchen sink.

"I'm not a tour guide," Ian grumbled.

The kettle whistled and Fiona stood back up to make tea. "I brought scones. Will you have one?"

Ian shook his head.

"Did you offer that poor girl anything to drink or eat?" his sister asked.

"No."

"Did you lose your manners along with your career?" she challenged. She was the only person who could get away with talking to him like that.

His expression went dark as he stared at her. He wasn't the hospitality sector.

What he'd feared, Fiona was now doing: bringing down three mugs and three plates. Ian sighed. Now they would be forced to make inane conversation.

"She's pretty, isn't she? Her hair is such a gorgeous shade. I'm envious," Fiona said, and she laid the plates down on the table. "A lot of women pay big money in the salons to get their hair that particular shade of red."

Ian shrugged. He wasn't going to be baited into admitting he found Johanna attractive. Even if he did.

Fiona opened the door to the sitting room. "Jo, would you join us for a cuppa?"

Jo hesitated, but Fiona encouraged her. "You must be thirsty."

"All right then," Jo said, following Fiona into the kitchen.

She was pretty, Ian thought. Wholesome looking. Unaffected. Words like *do-gooder* and *Pollyanna* came to mind.

"Jo, you've done a great job. Why don't you sit down? I've brought scones for us," Fiona said. She threw her brother a look. "I'm sorry, my brother seems to have forgotten his manners."

"No problem," Jo said. She pulled up a chair and sat across from Ian at the table.

Was she always in a good mood? Ian wondered. He didn't know if he could stand it. It was going to be a long month.

Fiona pushed the plate of scones toward Jo. "Help yourself."

"Thank you," Jo said, reaching for a raisin scone and placing it on her plate.

"Would you like lemon curd or jam with it?" Fiona asked, carrying the pot of tea over to the table and setting it on a hot plate.

Jo frowned and asked, "What's lemon curd?"

"It's a dessert spread. It always reminds me of lemon meringue pie," Fiona said, returning to the other side of the kitchen. She pulled a jar each of strawberry jam and lemon curd from the top shelf and brought them back to the table.

"Ian, pour the tea, unless your fingers are broken." Fiona handed Jo a teaspoon. "Try the lemon curd, you might like it."

Jo plunged her spoon into the curd and helped herself to a generous portion. Ian raised another eyebrow and wondered when she last ate. And where she put it all.

"That's delish," Jo said.

Delish?

"You're right, it tastes like lemon meringue pie," Jo said brightly.

"Doesn't it?" Fiona looked at her brother and smiled.

Ian could tell that Fiona liked Jo. He hoped his sister wouldn't start getting notions into her head and playing matchmaker. All three of his siblings had loved doing that in the past, and never more than during his career as a rugby player. They had more friends, and those friends had sisters . . . The breadth and depth of it was unimaginable. There had been no takers in the last few months, he thought bitterly.

"What do you do in your spare time, Jo?" Fiona asked as she fixed her own cup of tea.

Jo buttered up her scone and put a liberal amount of lemon curd on top of it. "I love to sketch and paint, mostly watercolors, but I'm hoping to learn oils as well."

Fiona raised her eyebrows. "Did you go to school for this?"

Jo blushed. "No, it's more of a hobby."

"You've come to the right place to sketch things," Fiona said and then with a look to her brother, she added, "Don't you think so, Ian?"

He shrugged. "I suppose."

"Ian could take you up to the castle tomorrow if you'd like to see that. Maybe do some sketching."

Jo's gaze landed on Ian's. "If you don't mind . . ."

What was he going to say? He wasn't a total jerk.

"You'll have to drive," he finally said. He could practically feel the triumph emanating off his sister.

Jo bit her lip. "That would mean driving on the opposite side of the road . . ."

"And the driver sits on the opposite side of the car," Ian added helpfully. Maybe there was a way out after all.

Before Jo could protest, Fiona said, "Ah, sure, you'll be grand."

Jo appeared doubtful.

Fiona added, "You'll be fine, you'll see. Lots of tourists drive all over the country." When Jo laughed, Fiona added, "That's great. You're all set."

Ian did not miss the look of self-satisfaction on his sister's face.

Chapter Seven

AT BREAKFAST THE FOLLOWING morning, Bridie was delighted when she heard Ian was going to take Jo sightseeing. She and Gram exchanged a knowing look. But Jo was less convinced. She had the impression that Ian had been strong-armed into it by Fiona. Although it had been Bridie's idea for Jo to help Ian out, she certainly didn't want to be a burden to anyone. If Ian bristled at the thought of her companionship—or worse, felt it was forced companionship—then Jo feared it might be all for naught.

Despite all these misgivings, Jo went into it with an open mind, and admittedly, some excitement about finally seeing something in Ireland. Just hanging around had made her bored. Gram and Bridie did their own thing, and Jo didn't want to be a third wheel. It was not lost on her that Gram and Bridie had already been doing a lot more than she had. Hopefully, today would remedy that situation.

Once she was dressed and had done her hair and put on a little makeup, she packed up her backpack with her sketch pad and pencils and headed off to Ian's house. Gram and Bridie had already left for the day to join a group from town on a bus trip up to the shrine at Knock, a three-hour journey each way. Bridie had invited her, but while the part about stopping for meals and the promise of a rowdy, song-filled return journey sounded interesting, Jo hadn't really wanted to go there. A religious shrine was not at the top of her list of places to visit. It would be a day spent attending Mass, lighting candles, saying a Rosary, browsing the gift shop, and buying lots of Mass cards. That wasn't what she came to Ireland for.

Jo knocked on the door and waited. Where would Ian take her, she wondered. With her back to the door, she looked down the footpath toward the road. The Twomeys lived outside of town center and on the way in, she and Gram had passed several interesting-looking shops and boutiques, which Jo had tucked away at the back of her mind to check out.

When there was no answer, she rapped on the door again, this time a little harder. It opened and Ian stood there, supported by his crutches.

"Good morning, Ian," she said with a smile.

"Yeah."

His enthusiasm was underwhelming.

He turned away from her and headed back into his home. Over his shoulder, he said, "Come on in, Johanna."

She followed him in. The sitting room was darkened; the drapes were still closed. He sat down on the sofa. Jo remained standing. She didn't want to sit down. She didn't want to get comfortable. She *wanted* to get moving.

"Are you ready?" she asked. She had an inkling that he was just getting up, even if it was late morning.

Ian sighed. "Yeah, about that. I don't think I'm up for that today."

"Okay," she said. As much as she tried, she couldn't hide her disappointment. The mood she had arrived in, a good one, quickly disappeared.

When he didn't add anything, Jo decided she wasn't going to change his mind. She wasn't going to force him. Maybe it was time she went off and did some things by herself. There must be a tour bus she could catch. There needed to be another conversation with Bridie about Jo's role with Ian. It appeared it wasn't going to work.

"How come?" she asked.

"How come what?"

"What changed your mind?" she asked. He still hadn't moved.

He shrugged, not looking at her. Staring at the ceiling. "I don't know. Just don't feel like it."

"Exhausted from everything you did yesterday? Full schedule of activities today?" she asked.

Even in the semi-darkness of the room, she could see him narrowing his eyes at her. She didn't care. She wasn't going to pressure him into doing anything, that wasn't her style, but she wasn't going to let him off the hook that easy.

"I changed my mind," he said tightly.

"Hmm," Jo said. With a nod toward his ankle, she swallowed hard and said, "I think you use that injury as an excuse so you don't have to deal with things, namely moving on with your life."

The air immediately became charged, as if a thunderstorm were rolling in.

"Excuse me?" he said.

"Ian, you made a promise last night, and it seems as if your word means nothing." She didn't care if he was offended. She'd quit her job to come all this way, and she was not going to spend the whole once-in-a-lifetime vacation sitting around inside Bridie's house. Seriously, she thought, she might never get the chance to come back to Ireland.

"Maybe tomorrow we can do something," he grumbled.

"Have a great day, Ian," she said as she turned on her heel and exited his house.

She heard him call out, "Johanna . . ."

Chapter Eight

WHEN THE DOOR CLOSED behind Jo, Ian bent his head. Everything she'd said was right and true, and yet it seemed almost a Herculean effort to leave the house. He didn't think he could do it.

He sat there in the darkened room for a while, thinking about the way his life *used* to be before the accident. Back then, he'd never been home. It was only a place to sleep and get changed. He'd been busy all day with either training, matches, or charity events. And then there was all the traveling. And the nights were spent going out. Or taking a pretty girl, someone like Jo, out and about. Jo *was* pretty, but he had to be honest with himself. Before, he probably wouldn't have taken a girl like her out. He would have noticed her all right—how could you not with that beautiful red hair?—but he'd have gone for someone more glamorous. There was a bitter taste in his mouth as he realized how shallow he must have been.

When Nana found out later that he'd abandoned Jo, he'd never hear the end of it. He sighed, frustrated. She liked to draw or paint or something like that. There were old church ruins just outside of town, and tomorrow was supposed to be dry. He supposed he could do something like that, if only to keep his grandmother off his back.

He was alone. He had the whole day to get used to the idea of leaving his house tomorrow. Work himself up to it. Talk himself into it. It would be a short trip, and he could sit in the car while she wandered the ruins. It made no difference whether he sat in his car or in his house.

After a while, somewhat pleased with this plan, he got on his crutches and headed over to the front window, pulling open the drapes and letting the daylight in.

At some point later, he'd make his way down to his Nana's house and tell Jo the plan for the next day.

After Jo left Ian's house, she headed toward the town center, thinking she could spend the day checking out the town and maybe stop to grab a bite to eat for lunch. Her plan was to look into tours. Surely there had to be a bus or train she could catch somewhere. Later tonight, she would have an honest talk with Bridie about how this scheme of hers just wasn't going to work. She'd talk to her own grandmother privately if need be. There was no sense in beating a dead horse.

The town center was a series of two- and three-story terraced houses, some private homes and some converted to shops, boutiques, and restaurants or cafés. Christmas music played from speakers on the street corners, and the shop windows were decorated with lights, garlands, ornaments, or a big wreath. Lights were strung from one side of the street to the other. An impressive Christmas tree stood in the town square next to the fountain, laden with lights. Jo made a note to stroll down after dark; she'd like to see it then. She walked the narrow footpath, careful not to jostle other pedestrians. Everyone was so friendly. People either nodded as they passed or made a comment about the weather—"It's a nice, fresh day,"—or simply said hello.

A small river circled the outside of the town center, and Jo managed to find stairs that led down toward it. A footpath ran parallel to the river, and Jo found a bench to sit on. On the other side of the river, up at the top of the riverbank, was a church, a gray stone affair with a tall, narrow steeple. She decided she might want to try and sketch that. She usually favored drawing people, as she loved the nuanced expressions, but she enjoyed sketching scenery and landscapes as well.

Once situated on the bench, she pulled out her sketch pad and pencil kit from her backpack and leaned back, crossing her legs. She found a blank page and went to work, her eyes darting back and forth between the church and its spire and the page before her. She was distracted at first by people walking by on the footpath, but it wasn't long before she found her focus and got lost in her sketching. She didn't become aware of the time again until it began to sprinkle. She looked up and saw that the sky had gone dark toward the east. Deciding it was best to move on, she packed up her things and closed her backpack. With her phone, she took a picture of the church, in case she didn't make it back or she found some down time at Bridie's to work on her drawing. As she exited the footpath onto the main thoroughfare her stomach growled, and she went in search of something to eat.

At the top of the town center, she spotted a sign for a café and headed toward it.

It was a small place with a smattering of tables and chairs. A counter with stools ran the length of the front window.

Jo studied the menu for a moment before placing an order for a toasted sandwich, a piece of chocolate cake, and a large coffee. She settled in at the counter at the window to eat and people-watch, one of her favorite pastimes. She reflected on how odd it felt to be in another country at Christmastime and not working her retail job. It appeared it wasn't going to work out as far as Ian was concerned, but that was all right; she was going to make the most of it. Displayed on the end of the counter were various travel brochures advertising area day trips. She selected a bunch and began to peruse them. It turned out she was interested in seeing a lot of different things. There was an art museum not far off, and that would be the first call she'd be making. Maybe she could make arrangements for tomorrow. A day trip to Dublin might also be in order. She could take the bus up and be back by nighttime. She was starting to get excited. Just because it hadn't worked out with Ian didn't mean she couldn't still have a good time here in Ireland.

Feeling better, she finished her meal and headed back toward Bridie's house. It was beginning to get dark, and she didn't want to be walking around on her own. She didn't want to get lost.

Bridie's house was still dark by the time she landed. There were lights on at Ian's house, but Jo wasn't going there. Bridie had said they wouldn't be back until eight or nine, but she had shown Jo where the spare key was kept. She retrieved it, unlocked the front door, and returned the key to its secret hiding place.

She turned on the light in the sitting room and made herself comfortable. The dog, Scruff, wandered out from the kitchen and wagged his tail when he spotted Jo. After he tried and failed several times to get up onto the sofa, Jo picked him up and placed him on the cushion next to her. The dog ran around in a circle three or four times before settling down and curling up on the cushion.

Jo pulled out her sketch pad; she wanted to put some finishing touches on her drawing from earlier. While she was digging through her backpack for her phone, she heard the front door open. Thinking it was Gram and Bridie, she jumped up off the sofa and headed out of the sitting room. But she pulled up short when she saw that it was Ian.

"Oh, it's you," she blurted.

"Sorry to disappoint you," he said.

Jo realized it hadn't sounded the way she meant it. "No, I meant I wasn't expecting you."

"No worries. Look, I was wondering if you were up to going to see some ruins or something tomorrow." He leaned on both crutches.

"Did you want to sit down?" she asked.

He shook his head. "No, I'm not staying. I just came down here to see if you wanted to do some sightseeing tomorrow. Bring your sketchbook or something."

Jo wondered if he'd change his mind by the morning and bail on her.

"Look, I promise I won't cancel on you," he said.

"All right."

"You'll have to drive, though," he said, turning around, his hand on the door.

"What time?"

Ian made sure he was ready by the time Jo showed up the following morning. He opened the front door before she had a chance to knock. He did not miss the look of surprise on her face. He was surprised himself.

"Good morning, Johanna, I'm all set," he said. He handed her the car keys.

She looked nice: she had a winter coat on over jeans, and she wore a pair of short-heeled boots. Her auburn curls escaped from a knitted hat with a pom-pom on top, just reaching her shoulders.

Ian locked the house behind him and as they headed down the footpath to his car, parked in the street, he said to her, "All right, any conditions?"

She frowned. "Conditions? What do you mean?"

"Like you don't want to be outside because it's too damp, or you don't want to drive too far."

"Oh, that." She appeared thoughtful for a moment. "The only condition I would have is that we have to stop somewhere to eat. Because if I get hangry it won't be a pleasant experience for either one of us."

"Okay, so you need to be fed and watered regularly."

"Please."

At the curb, they both went for the right-side door of Ian's car.

"What are you doing?" Ian asked. "You're driving."

Jo looked at him and then looked at the car. It took a moment, but she finally said, "Nothing. Never mind."

She headed to the other side, and Ian couldn't help but wonder about her driving ability.

When she slid into the driver's seat, she familiarized herself with the interior. Her gaze landed on the stick shift between the two seats, and she frowned.

"What's wrong?" Ian asked.

"Is that a stick shift?"

"It is."

"I don't know how to drive a manual. I only know how to drive an automatic."

And with that, Ian burst out laughing.

Once he pulled himself together, Ian realized that an opportunity had landed in his lap. If Jo couldn't drive a manual, there'd be no way for him to show her around Ireland. He was off the hook. From here on out, they could go their separate ways.

"Well, that's that," Ian said, triumphant over this unexpected bonus. He opened the door and made to get out. His mood had improved tenfold.

He'd just stepped his good foot out onto the street when Jo said from the driver's seat behind him, "Why can't you teach me to drive a stick shift?"

Ian closed his eyes and sighed. She would ask that. First, they expected him to be a tour guide. Now she wanted him to be a driving instructor. What was tomorrow? Teach her how to play rugby? It was going to be never ending.

Jo hadn't budged from the driver's seat. *Don't turn around, don't look at her. Don't do it!* But what did he do? He turned around to be met with a smiling Jo, who raised an eyebrow at him. He chided himself for being so weak that he'd do whatever a pretty girl asked him to do.

"I'm a quick learner," she added with a grin. He wondered if there was a boyfriend back home; there must be. Where had that thought come from?

He held firm. "Sorry, I'm not a driving instructor."

He hoisted himself out of the car onto the street and limped around to the back seat to grab his crutches, ignoring Jo. She could sit in the car for the rest of the day, but he wasn't going to cave. Teaching her how to drive wasn't part of the agreement.

When he reached his front door, he realized Jo was following him. With his back to her, he rolled his eyes. She was turning into a barnacle.

"Look, Ian, I don't mean to be a pain in the neck," she started.

Before he could respond, someone shouted out, "Ian!"

When Ian saw who it was, he sighed. Frank, the physical therapist. The one he'd been purposefully avoiding.

"Hey, Ian, what's the craic?" Frank asked.

"Nothing," Ian replied, fumbling to get his key in the door. He was anxious to get away from both Frank and Johanna.

"I thought so," Frank said grimly. "I've been texting and leaving messages, but you haven't returned my calls."

Ian shrugged. By not averting his gaze from Frank, he felt as if he was challenging him. He was also aware of Jo, standing there, observing the interaction.

"Anyway, you probably want to get started on your rehab so you can get your ankle back in top shape," Frank said.

"Will it get me back onto the field?" Ian asked.

Jo's eyes went as big as saucers. But Ian didn't care. He wasn't the nice police. And if she didn't like it, she could leave. But she remained rooted to the spot.

"It's a start to rebuilding your life," Frank said.

"What life?" Ian asked. Hadn't Johanna said the same thing to him the previous night? Everyone seemed to be singing from the same hymn sheet.

"You'll be able to carve out a new life," Frank pointed out.

"I had a life," Ian spat. "I want that life back. I don't want a new one! I want to have the life I had!"

"Okay," Frank said.

"Okay, what? You'll get me my old life back?" Ian said. "If I go through all this physical therapy, will I be able to go back and play for my team? That was my life. Rugby was my life. The Irish Rovers were my life. It was my career. That's all gone now. All gone in the past. My life is over!"

Ian glanced over at Jo, whose eyes were still wide with something akin to shock registering on her face. His anger now propelling him forward, he turned on her. "And I don't want your company. You're only here because of pity."

She didn't move. He squeezed his eyes shut. When he opened them, Jo and Frank were staring at him. Neither appeared uncomfortable at his outburst. How much did you have to do to insult people?

Maybe they wouldn't leave, but he could. He fumbled his key in the lock and finally managed to get the door open. He stepped inside. Before he closed the door he said, "No need for either one of you to stay. I'm fine by myself."

CHAPTER NINE

J O STOOD THERE ON the footpath outside Ian's home. The physical therapist shrugged and walked away. Her gaze bounced from Bridie's house back to Ian's. Here she was in one of the most beautiful countries in the world, and she had yet to see anything. Jo watched the physical therapist get in his car and drive away, then sighed and headed back to Bridie's house to regroup.

Bridie and Gram were gone for the day, but Jo had to find something to do. She didn't even know how to turn the television on. Thinking she had plans with Ian, she hadn't booked any of the tours she'd read about in the café. Finally, she decided she'd try catching a bus and seeing where she ended up.

Two blocks from Bridie's house, Jo had seen a bus stop. She made sure she had her wallet and sketch pad in her backpack and hoofed it up there. She studied the schedule posted behind an acrylic casing at the stop. There was a bus going to Enniscorthy in ten minutes. She nodded to herself. That's where she'd go. It was likely to be a much bigger town than the one Bridie lived in so ideally, she could spend the day there and be back in the evening. She hoped there were things to see. Although the sky was dull, it was dry, and Jo hoped the rain would hold off.

The bus for Enniscorthy rolled in right on time and Jo boarded it, paid for a round-trip ticket, and took a seat at the back.

Enniscorthy indeed turned out to be a large town, and Jo figured she'd need more than an afternoon to explore it, but she made the best of the time she had. First, she walked around the town to get a feel for it and ended up walking by the River Slaney. She thought she'd like to come back and sketch it properly if she had time. But she headed back toward town center and found herself drawn to Enniscorthy Castle, spending more than an hour exploring it. She questioned one of the docents about tours of the town and was directed to an outfit that did walking tours. Jo thought she might like that, so she signed up for a walking tour that was two hours long. Afterward, she stopped at a café for a bite to eat and some tea, careful with her money because she didn't have a lot of it. At least she didn't have to worry about buying presents, as she did her Christmas shopping all through the year. Her gifts were currently wrapped and sitting beneath her parents' tree back home.

At the end of the day, she sank into her seat at the back of the bus, exhausted from all the walking. There was only one time she'd pulled out her sketch pad. She was tired in a good way and was looking forward to going back and catching up with her grandmother. She knew Gram was having a good time. She'd been all smiles when they went to bed the night before and had been asleep in seconds.

As she watched the scenery passing by from her seat on the bus, Jo was glad she'd been brave enough to get out and go see something, even though she would have preferred to see these things with someone else. It wasn't ideal to have no one to talk to, no one to share it with.

By the time she arrived back at Bridie's, it was dark out, and Jo decided that she'd venture up to Dublin the next day. She'd looked up the bus schedule and if she got down to the bus stop early enough, she could make a day of it. She could make some sandwiches and carry them in her backpack. That would solve the problem of spending too much money on food.

Bridie's house was dark, which indicated that Gram and Bridie weren't back yet. They'd gone visiting some friends. Once inside, Jo dropped her coat, scarf, and backpack in the room she was sharing with Gram. She'd just gone to the sitting room and turned the light on when the front door opened and Bridie and Gram came through, loud and giggling.

Jo couldn't help but smile. The most important thing was for Gram to be enjoying herself.

"Oh, there you are, Jo," Gram said.

"Hi, Gram," Jo said, giving her grandmother a hug. She always loved the way her grandmother smelled: something lemony. "Did you have a good day?"

"It was wonderful! I met up with people I haven't seen in fifty years!" Gram's eyes sparkled, and Jo thought she should have brought her over much sooner.

"We had a lot of laughs, reminiscing about the old days," Bridie chimed in. "What did you do today, Jo?"

"I went to Enniscorthy," Jo said. "Spent the day there. Loved it."

Bridie's eyes widened. "Enniscorthy? How did you get Ian to go to Enniscorthy?"

Jo shook her head and blushed. "Oh no, I'm sorry. I went by myself. I took the bus."

Bridie looked puzzled. "I thought Ian was taking you somewhere today."

Jo gave a small smile. "I don't know how to drive a stick shift."

Bridie pressed her lips together until they disappeared. "So he left you to your own devices?"

"Oh, it's all right," Jo said hurriedly. She certainly didn't want to get Ian into trouble. "Everything turned out fine."

"I'll be right back," Bridie said, and she disappeared from the sitting room.

Jo sank onto the sofa and put her head in her hands. "Oh, Gram, what have I agreed to? Ian Twomey doesn't want any company!"

Gram sat next to her and patted her hand. "Don't worry about it, Jo, it was just an idea. Bridie so wants to help Ian, but you can't help someone who doesn't want to be helped."

"I can't take any money from Bridie. It wouldn't be right."

"I'll talk to Bridie, and you're not to worry about money while we're here," Gram reassured her.

"I'm so sorry," Jo said.

"Johanna, this is your trip as much as it is mine," Gram said. "And I know how much you gave up to come here with me."

"I do love it here, though, Gram, and I'm so glad I came with you," Jo said. She didn't want her grandmother feeling bad about anything.

"I'm glad to hear that. Now tomorrow, Bridie and I are taking the bus down to Kilkenny with the garden club, but maybe the day after would be a good day to visit my homeplace."

"Oh, I'd love that," Jo said.

"What will you do tomorrow?" Gram asked.

"I thought I might take the bus into Dublin and spend the day there."

"Good." Gram stood up and reached for her handbag. She dug out her wallet and pulled out some euro notes.

"No, Gram, I'm not taking your money," Jo protested.

"Nonsense. Dublin is expensive, and I want you to have a good time," Gram said, urging her to take the notes.

"I will have a good time," Jo said. "I'm going to pack myself a picnic."

"*Pah*! You're on vacation. You're not brown-bagging it," Gram said. "Now treat yourself to a nice meal while you're there. You might want to check out the National Gallery of Ireland. They have beautiful works of art there."

"I will," Jo said. Her grandmother pushed the notes into Jo's hand, and Jo sighed. "All right, Gram, thanks. But this is just a loan."

Gram shook her head. "Not at all. It's a gift."

Chapter Ten

"Ian, what happened while Mary and I were away today?" Nana demanded. She stood with her hands on her hips, scowling, and the tone of her voice was enough to make Ian sit up straighter. He'd never seen her so furious. Not even when he was fifteen and he'd taken her car and picked up his friends and gone joyriding. He didn't know what she was so angry about. Yet. It was either Johanna or Frank. Jo must have squealed on him, told her how he'd ditched her and turned the physical therapist away.

In his mind, he went over the conversation with Jo earlier that day. If he'd insulted or offended her, he didn't know when he did it or what he'd said. It wasn't his fault that she didn't know how to drive a manual. With lack of a car and driver out of the equation, he wouldn't have to entertain her. Or she him. The reality of that had improved his mood. That is, until his grandmother came storming in. He couldn't help but notice there was no plate of sandwiches in her hand.

"What did Johanna say I said to her?" he asked, feeling his own ire rising. Jo, as sweet as she appeared, was a troublemaker if she'd gone crying to his grandmother about him.

"She didn't say one word against you. Only that she took the bus to Enniscorthy by herself!"

Ian sighed. He didn't say anything. He didn't have to, for Nana took over.

"Never in the history of tourists visiting Ireland has someone been treated so poorly!" his grandmother raged. "The Irish are noted all around the world for our hospitality, but you can't even manage that!"

It was best to remain silent.

"Mary is worried about Jo, and I don't want her worrying about anything!" Nana said. "I was so looking forward to seeing my best friend. It'll probably be the last time we see each other in our lifetimes . . ." Her voice trailed off.

Ian pressed his lips together. Boy, she was shrewd.

His gaze landed on his sitting room. The artificial tree in the front window, sparkling with multicolored lights and laden with ornaments. The candle that smelled like pinecones. The various holiday decorations placed throughout the room. An American girl had come over to Ireland and spent part of her holiday getting his home ready for Christmas. And had he thanked her? No. He hadn't even offered her so much as a cup of tea. He sighed. His sister was right. It appeared he'd lost his manners along the way.

"I don't ask for much, Ian," Nana said softly.

Ian blew out a breath. He supposed it was only for one month. Surely he could put up with Jo for one month?

"All right, you win," he muttered.

"You've got two choices. Either hire a taxi and take her around, or teach her how to drive your car," Nana said.

Ian said nothing.

"I'm waiting," Nana said.

He thought about it for a moment. "I'll teach her how to drive my car."

"Good. I'll send her up by ten tomorrow morning. She's usually up by nine, but I'll give you until ten," Nana said. "And you'd better be polite."

He grumbled beneath his breath.

"Don't give me any cheek," she scolded. "And what's this I hear you turned Frank away?"

Ian exploded. "Did she tell you that too? Probably couldn't wait to tell you!"

His grandmother paled. "No, Frank rang me while I was away trying to enjoy myself."

That was the problem with living next door to family. They were in your business all the time.

"He's wasting his time coming here," Ian muttered.

"You're wasting his time by not letting him do his job," Nana countered.

His grandmother stood at the door before him. Her face was shrinking and it startled him. When had she gotten so old-looking? He took it for granted that his nan would be around forever. But one bitter lesson that life had taught him was that nothing lasted forever.

"What happened to you is tragic, there is no other way to say it," Nana started.

Ian couldn't look at her.

"And I know you're angry. It's understandable because you've lost a lot," she said. "But you have to move on with your life. Carve out a new path for yourself."

"I am moving on," Ian mumbled. But even as he said it, he knew his statement had a lot of holes in it.

Nana shook her head. "This isn't moving on. This is hiding. This is giving up. This is not having the guts to face what happened and overcome it."

"Am I not allowed to grieve?" he asked, his voice rising.

"Of course you're allowed to grieve for what you've lost! But you can't grieve forever. You're too young, and you have a lot of life ahead of you yet," Nana said.

"That's the unfortunate part. I wish it had been a more serious accident," he admitted. He stared at his hands in his lap. "One that I wouldn't have survived."

The color drained from Nana's face. "Don't ever say that. Promise me that you'll never do anything like that. That you'll reach out for help if you need it," she said, her voice breaking.

Ian hated himself for worrying his grandmother. No matter how angry he was, she didn't deserve that. "No, Nana, I won't." To reassure her, he added, "I promise."

His grandmother recovered her composure and appeared her old, formidable self. "You can get your own supper tonight. There's too much coddling going on around here. Your hands aren't broken. Make your own sandwiches."

His grandmother loved to feed people. It told him the degree of her anger if she was going to force him to make his own supper. But deep down, he knew she was right.

After Nana left, Ian thought about things and resigned himself to his fate with Jo. He blew out a long sigh. Why couldn't everyone just leave him alone?

"Okay, Johanna, don't be nervous," Ian told Jo from his position in the passenger seat. The day was dreary, the sky charcoal gray with a continual mist. It didn't help with his current mood. He'd been up early in the morning, anxious to get going and get it over with.

"I'm not nervous," Jo said.

"Then why are you shaking?" he asked, nodding toward her trembling hands on the steering wheel.

"Oh." Jo folded her hands in her lap.

It had been a little awkward for the two of them when they'd first met up earlier that morning. She looked as if she wanted to spend time with him as much as he did with her, and she most likely knew that his grandmother had strong-armed him into being nice. He decided to ignore it and was relieved when she chose that option as well.

In the confined space of the car, Ian could smell her perfume, something that reminded him of vanilla. Up close, he could see her hazel eyes were greener, with flecks of brown and gold. Her hair appeared much darker. He was certain there must be a boyfriend back home.

It was amazing how he'd lost his confidence along with his career. Before, he would have enjoyed being with Johanna just because she was female. He would have engaged in some harmless flirting. He wondered if she would have been shy around him. But now, unsure of the landscape, he didn't know how the opposite sex would react to him. And he didn't want to test it out. Not now and maybe not ever.

"Should I put the key in the ignition?" Jo asked, breaking his train of thought. He snapped out of it and looked at her. She was staring at him but turned away when his eyes met hers.

Ian coughed. "Yes. Now, see the three pedals there. Going left to right, you've got your clutch, your brake, and your petrol pedal."

Jo turned her attention to her feet. "Uh-huh."

"Here's the stick, this is how you change gears," he said, taking hold of the gearshift in the center of the console between the front seats. He shifted up and to the left for first, straight down for second, up for third, down for fourth, and then back up and further right for fifth, explaining as he demonstrated. "You'll start out in first after you take off the emergency brake."

Jo didn't say anything, just kept nodding.

"Now, here's the tricky part," he said. "As you're shifting gears, you step down on the clutch with your left foot."

"Okay," she said and then repeated in a whisper, "When shifting gears, step down on the clutch."

"You're going to be fine," he said.

She looked up at him with her big hazel eyes, and she appeared doubtful.

"Do you know, Johanna, most people in Ireland drive manual as opposed to automatic," he said.

"Really? Why?" she asked.

Ian shrugged. "Who knows?" Automatic would certainly be easier, but that's the way it was.

"Okay, so start the car, put your right foot on the brake, and take the emergency brake off," he instructed, indicating the brake lever on the mid console behind the stick shift.

Once that was done, she waited for his next instruction.

God, she was pretty. He wanted to touch her hair. It looked so shiny and silky. His eyes landed on her lips, soft and full. He wondered what it would feel like to kiss them. He cleared his throat and frowned. "Now very firmly, step down on the clutch and shift into first gear."

With an intense frown of concentration, Jo stared down at the stick shift and put her left foot down on the clutch. She tried shifting into first gear, but took her foot off the clutch too soon, causing the car to lurch forward then stall out. Ian winced.

"No worries. That happens to everybody. Don't take your foot off the clutch until you've engaged the gear. Once the gear is engaged, you'll use your right foot to gently step on the petrol pedal while easing your foot off the clutch."

She nodded and went for the stick shift. He reached out and placed his hand over hers. Her hand was soft and delicate beneath his.

"Wait a minute," he said. "Turn the car off for a moment."

She turned the key in the ignition and said, "I told you I couldn't do it." She sank back in the seat, defeated, pulling her hand away.

He laughed. "Johanna, cool down. I had you turn off the car because I want you to get used to the stick shift."

"Hmm."

"Yeah, hmm," he repeated. "Grab hold of that shift. Now just move it around from gear to gear. That's right, go down to second, and can you feel how it catches and locks into place? That's right. Start with first, down to second, back up to third, which you'll note is between first and fifth."

Jo worked at changing gears over and over. After a while, she nodded. Ian studied her: the curl of hair hanging loose from her ponytail. The little furrow of concentration between her eyebrows as she focused on her task. He was trying to picture her in her own environment. But he couldn't. His brain kept bringing her back to Ireland. Although Ireland's scenery was beautiful, Johanna certainly added to it.

She practiced a few times, repeating his instructions in a whisper, her face a portrait of concentration.

"Will we give it a go?" he asked.

Her head snapped up. "Right now?"

"Yeah, sure, no time like the present," he said.

"I thought I'd practice this for a bit," she said.

He shook his head. "Just that? And what would be for tomorrow? Turning the key in the ignition?"

"Well, no," she said. She started up the car and looked in the side and rearview mirrors.

"Okay, right foot on the brake, release the emergency brake, put your left foot down on the clutch, and shift into first." He added, "Don't take your foot off the clutch until you're in first."

Johanna did what she was told, and everything seemed perfect until she stepped on the gas pedal. The car lurched forward and then came to an abrupt halt again.

"No worries," Ian said reassuringly. "Just need a smoother transition."

"Do you think?" Johanna asked.

After several attempts, she finally got going and the car lurched forward, sputtered, and began heading toward town center.

Johanna's eyes grew wide. "You're not going to have me drive in traffic, are you?"

"Nope, you're going to take this first right here. It will take us away from the town."

She nodded. After a quick search, she put on the indicator. She was still driving in first gear. Once she made the turn, they headed away from the town center.

"All right, we can't drive in first gear forever, so as soon as you feel the gear tugging, step on the clutch and shift into second."

Johanna nodded her head quickly, dragging her eyes away from the road to look at the stick shift.

"Don't forget your clutch," Ian reminded her.

"Got it."

Johanna stepped on the clutch and shifted gears. The car sputtered and stalled out.

"Or you could skip second and just go on to third," Ian noted with amusement.

"Did I skip second?" she asked, restarting the car.

"You did. Shift down for second. I should have reminded you."

Once the car was started, she shifted into first, and the vehicle moved forward in a smooth motion.

"Good, you're getting first gear sorted. Only four more to go."

She gave him a tentative smile.

He cleared his throat and stared straight ahead. He didn't want to look at her and think again how attractive she was. There was no point in it. The prospect of nothing would only further depress him.

"As you pick up speed, Johanna, shift down into second," he said.

Jo followed his instruction. It was a rough transition, but the car didn't stall.

"Okay, good," he said. "Pick up speed a bit, and you're going to step on the clutch and shift into third."

His eyes widened as she veered over to the wrong side of the road. "Whoa, remember, we drive on the left side of the road here."

"Oh jeez, there's so much to remember."

He'd keep a close eye on her and the road.

He directed her away from town center, where the traffic was light, and Jo got much better at driving the manual and navigating the narrow roads—there was only one near-miss with a tractor where Jo plowed straight into a hedge on the side of the road.

They'd been driving for three quarters of an hour, and Jo's confidence was starting to improve when Ian spotted a familiar landmark up ahead.

"What is that?" Jo asked.

"That's Tintern Abbey, or what's left of it," he told her.

"Can we stop?" she asked.

He was just about to say no. He'd driven by this abbey many times in his life and had never felt compelled to stop.

She looked over at him, a look of excitement on her face. He supposed he couldn't just give her a driving lesson and call it a day.

"Sure," he found himself saying.

He directed her to where to park the car. Once she turned the car off, she opened the door and jumped out. She grabbed her backpack from behind the seat. From the back seat, she asked him, "Aren't you coming?"

He shook his head. "Nah, I'll wait here."

"Really?"

"Yeah, I'm good. Take your time, Johanna, no rush," he advised.

"I will, thanks," she said, and she closed the door.

When she hadn't returned half an hour later, Ian began to get irritated. How long did it take to look at a pile of rocks? He gave her ten more minutes and then, muttering under his breath, he limped out of the car and grabbed his crutches.

He found Jo sitting on a low stone wall outside the abbey ruins. Her head was bent over her sketch pad in her lap. She was so focused on her task she never heard him approach her.

"Johanna?"

The pad flew out of Jo's lap, and her arms flailed as she screamed in fright. Ian had to suppress a grin.

"It's just me," he finally said.

"Sorry," she said. She picked up her sketch pad from where it had fallen. She looked up to the ruins, down to her pad, and then over to him. "I won't be much longer. I can take some pictures and finish it later."

"No, take your time," Ian told her. Although he was ready to go home, he didn't want to rush her. Using his crutches, he stepped closer to her. "Can I see?"

She bit her lip, but she turned the pad around so he could see it.

Ian blinked in surprise. It wasn't just a sketch by a hobbyist. It was so realistic. "Wow, that's amazing! Hey, go ahead and finish what you're doing. Don't let me interrupt."

A flush crept up from her neck to her cheeks. She nodded and went back to work with the pencils laid out beside her.

Ian walked around, taking his time on the crutches. He took a good look at the ruins and had to admit that it was pretty impressive that the site was almost nine hundred years old. He supposed there was something to be said for that.

Eventually, he made his way back to Jo and took a seat on the low stone wall. He realized he was in her way and went to move.

"No need to move," she said, not lifting her head. "I'm almost finished."

A few moments later, she folded her sketchbook closed and stuffed it into her backpack along with her tray of pencils.

"How long have you been drawing?" he asked, curious.

She shrugged. "For as long as I can remember. But when I was in high school, my art teacher really encouraged me."

"Is that what you do? Professionally, I mean?"

"Oh no, this is just a hobby."

By the looks of it, her talent had gone beyond hobby. "Do you go to college or do you work?"

She looked away. "I used to work in the mall, but I'm starting a new job at a coffee shop when I get back. The plan is to go to college once I figure out what I want to do with my life."

Ian didn't think it was any of his business to point out the obvious: that with that kind of talent, she should pursue an art degree.

She stood up and slung her backpack over her shoulder. "Ready?"

By the time they arrived back at the house, it was late afternoon. Ian had to admit that it was good to get out of the house, even if it was only for a drive and a stop to see some ruins. For the last few hours, he'd been concentrating so hard on teaching Jo how to drive that he hadn't given a thought to anything else, and it was a relief.

Ian told Jo to park the car on the road in front of the house, and they got out.

"Well, thank you," Jo said. "It wasn't as bad as I thought it would be."

"You're doing great," he said. Her cheeks went a tinge of pink, and Ian studied her for a moment. Before thinking about it, he blurted out, "Would you like to go to a pub later with me? I mean, I know it isn't much—"

"I'd love to," Jo said, smiling.

"Great, let's say eight o'clock?"

"All right, I'll see you then," she said.

CHAPTER ELEVEN

THERE WAS A SLIGHT mist in the air later that evening as Jo got ready to set out for the pub. She was looking forward to it. Before she left Bridie's house, she applied some lipstick and took one last look in the mirror. She loved going out at Christmastime; there was such a festive feeling in the air. She suspected it was probably the same way in Ireland. And she was hoping it would rub off on Ian. Or even a little of it.

The driving hadn't gone as bad as she had feared. It wasn't the driving itself that had worried her but being alone with Ian. Her experience so far was that he didn't want her company and was a bit of a grump. She couldn't blame him. But during the drive, he'd been okay. Almost friendly. More than once, she'd stolen a glance at him. That dark hair—she wondered if it was as soft as it looked. And she found herself fascinated by his beard. It worried Jo that she was having this kind of reaction to him. There were thousands of miles between them, and to harbor a crush on him would only lead to disappointment. Namely hers.

She shrugged on her coat and wrapped a green scarf around her neck.

In the kitchen, her grandmother huddled with Bridie over a springform pan. Something smelled good. The older women were whispering and giggling, unaware of her presence. Bridie was poking holes into the cake with a skewer.

"Don't be mean with the whiskey, Bridie." Gram laughed.

"I think you're right, Mary," Bridie said. She uncapped a bottle of Powers whiskey and poured some into each hole.

"What are you doing?" Jo asked, startling them, which resulted in more laughter.

"Making the Christmas cake," Bridie said.

Jo walked up to them and inspected the brown cake filled with sultanas, raisins, and dried fruit. The smell of whiskey assailed her nostrils.

She waved her hand in front of her nose. "A little strong on the booze, don't you think?"

Gram and Bridie exchanged a look and grinned.

"Do you add whiskey every day?" Jo asked, thinking her grandmother and Bridie would be bombed on fumes alone by the time Christmas rolled around.

Bridie's eyes widened. "Good Lord, no. We add it every ten days."

"How long ago did you make it?" Jo asked Bridie.

"I always make it six weeks ahead of Christmas," Bridie answered.

"And the alcohol is a preservative, so the cake keeps!" Gram enthused.

"I bet it does," Jo said wryly.

"Getting ready to head off?" Bridie asked.

"Yes, Ian said we'd go to the pub."

"It's a start," Bridie said with a nod of approval. "Although Jo, I disagree with you not taking any money for this."

Jo shook her head, relieved that Gram had spoken to Bridie. "I can't. We're just hanging out."

Bridie went to protest but Jo said, "Besides, I really don't mind."

The grandmothers glanced at each other and smiled. Jo frowned.

"I knew all he needed was a bit of company." Ian's grandmother beamed. "He's been so lonesome since the accident."

"Well, it's just a trip to the pub for a pint, so don't get too excited," Jo warned. She didn't want them to get their hopes up. She hated letting people down.

"Mary, Jo is the image of you at that age. I look at her and it's like I'm seeing you," Bridie said, her eyes filling up.

"What are you two getting up to this evening?" Jo said. She hoped it was something that didn't involve any more whiskey. She didn't want them turning maudlin or, worse, goofy.

"We're going to have some mince pies and watch the *Late, Late Show* tonight," Bridie said.

"I haven't seen the *Late, Late Show* since Gay Byrne hosted it," Mary said.

"May he rest in peace," Bridie added, making the sign of the cross.

Jo nodded. "That's great." She kissed her grandmother good-night and headed out into the mist.

She met Ian on the footpath just outside the house. She barely came up to his shoulder. His cologne was divine. Jo had to refrain from closing her eyes and drawing in a deep breath of it.

Ian seemed to study her for a moment before looking away quickly. He cleared his throat and asked, "Are you ready?"

She nodded.

"Would you mind carrying the umbrella?" he asked, holding it out to her.

"Nope," she said. "How far is it?"

"Not far. It's about a five-minute walk from here."

"Is it too much of a distance on crutches?" she asked tentatively.

Ian shook his head. "I can handle it."

"Or maybe I should drive," Jo debated.

"Come on, Johanna, let's go," Ian said.

The sky was dark. There were no stars or moon evident, which indicated heavy cloud cover. Although mild, the air was damp.

The walk toward town center was taking a bit longer than five minutes, and there was still no sign of a pub. Jo worried about Ian on the crutches, but he seemed to be managing. At least she had on comfortable boots with her skirt.

Looking around, she noticed that almost every window in the houses they passed had an electric candle in it. "What's that about? The candles in the windows?"

"That's an old Irish tradition. It's to light the way for the Holy Family or to let Joseph and Mary know that there's room in the home."

"That's lovely," Jo said. They went on in silence for a moment, and Jo studied all the houses and their varying Christmas decorations. It was just like back home, she thought. Festive and full of cheer. The color really helped with the dreary weather.

"Gram tells me you don't usually get snow in Ireland at Christmas. Is that the case?" she asked, hopeful he might disagree.

He nodded. "Yes. Sometimes we might get some in January. A few years back, we had a blizzard in March, practically shut down the country."

Jo didn't say anything. She liked the sound of Ian's voice or more specifically, his lilt.

The sky opened up and a torrent of rain fell upon them. It was so unexpected that Jo burst out laughing. Quickly, she opened the umbrella and held it over the both of them.

"Johanna, you don't have to hold the umbrella over my head. I don't mind a little water."

"A little water? It's biblical," she said.

Ian laughed. The rain battered the umbrella, cascading off the side of it. Jo could feel the rain soaking her leg. She noticed his arm was getting drenched.

"Oh no," Jo said.

"It'll pass," Ian said.

Jo's lower back was beginning to ache from the angle at which she had to hold the umbrella. "Should we go home?" she asked, not treasuring the thought of another night in.

"Not on your life." He stopped, resting on his crutches, and looked down at her legs, clad in black tights. "Come in closer, so you don't get soaked."

Jo felt a flush spread to her cheeks. She moved in next to him, mindful not to knock him off his crutches. With one hand holding the umbrella high above their heads, she adjusted her stride to match his.

"I hope it's quiet at the pub tonight. I really don't want to run into anyone I know," Ian said.

She wondered how realistic that was. He was a former rugby player who played for a national team. If Ireland was anything like the States, they'd know him as soon as he set foot in the pub.

She enjoyed the combination of his smell: soap, mint, and aftershave. It was heady.

"Are you all right?" he asked. "You have a strange look on your face."

"Yes, I'm fine," she said, keeping her eyes straight ahead.

"You're a funny bird, Johanna," Ian said.

When they reached the pub, Jo stared at Ian, who appeared not even to have broken a sweat covering the distance from his house to the pub on crutches. "Wow, your upper-body strength is amazing." She closed the umbrella.

Ian laughed and shook his head.

Jo felt her cheeks go scarlet.

The pub was located on a corner. Blinking lights decorated the windows of the white two-story building with orange trim, and green garland wrapped with blinking lights ran the length of the inside sill. On the side of the building, a sign painted in big, bold orange letters identified the place as "Keenan's." The door opened, and music and laughter spilled out. Two young men emerged. One of them, who looked to be in his early twenties, eyed Ian, nudged the other, and said, "It's Ian Twomey!"

Jo held her breath and Ian regarded them warily.

One of the men leaned toward Ian and extended his hand. "Great to see you out and about, mate."

"Thanks." Ian shook the man's hand and wished him a good night, and they headed down the street.

Ian paused at the now-closed pub door and appeared to hesitate. Before he could change his mind, Jo opened the door and held it for him.

Ian maneuvered the crutches up the step and nodded toward the umbrella stand.

"Just stick the brolly in there."

Jo frowned at the collection of plain black umbrellas in the stand, each one indistinguishable from the other. "How will we tell which one is ours when we're leaving?"

"We won't be able to, but we'll have an umbrella to go home. Come on, let's get a pint," he said. And then he muttered, "I might need one."

CHAPTER TWELVE

T HE FACE OF THE bartender, Johnny, lit up in recognition, and he shouted, "Ian! It's about time!"

Ian felt all the eyes in the pub turn toward him, and he wondered if this had been a good idea. The crowd at the bar parted, and he was able to make his way into the small space. Soon, he was crowded by patrons slapping him on the back and welcoming him. This was what he'd been afraid of, the reason he'd stayed in his house. Before, when he had his career, this had been his neighborhood pub. But it had been different then. Before, it was all about camaraderie. But now, he wasn't so sure. He didn't want their pity. He lost sight of Johanna, and a small sense of panic filled him. He felt something brush against his arm, and he looked down to see her standing next to him.

"I better hang on, or I'll get swallowed up." She winked at him. He smiled, glad she was there with him. It *seemed* normal. Two pints suddenly appeared as if by magic, and one was handed to Ian, the other to Johanna.

"It's on the house tonight, Ian," Johnny called. He nodded toward Jo. "For you and your girl."

Johanna smiled at the bartender and gave a little wave. "I'm Jo."

"You're very welcome, Jo." Johnny beamed. He went to the other end of the bar and announced, "Ian's back."

Despite all the attention, there was a part of Ian that was grateful Jo hadn't corrected Johnny about being his girl. He stroked his beard and thought about this.

Jo stood on her toes, the top of her head brushing against his chin. Her hair smelled like coconuts, and he was reminded of a tropical vacation. "There's a table over there," she said. "Would you prefer to sit there, or will we stay at the bar?"

"Actually, I would prefer that," he said. His armpits ached from the crutches. He'd like to give them a rest. Plus, it was crowded at the bar. He didn't want to be the center of attention, and he'd like to avoid any questions as to how he was doing.

Jo carried their pint glasses to an upholstered booth and scooted onto the leather bench seat. Ian set his crutches against the wall next to the booth and sat down next to Jo. Despite his anxiety, it did feel good to be out.

"So, Johanna, you said you'd be starting a new job when you return home?"

Jo nodded. "That's right. It's at a coffee shop within walking distance of where I live."

"That'll be handy."

"That's what I thought. The owners seemed nice when I went in for my interview. Definitely better than my former boss." She sipped her ale.

"Do you like customer service?" he asked. He was trying to picture her working an expensive coffee machine and dealing with all those complicated orders.

"I suppose I do. I like dealing with people."

"Is this what you want to do for the rest of your life?" he asked.

"I'm not sure what I want to do with the rest of my life," she said, not making eye contact but looking around the room. She regarded her pint glass. "I'm still trying to decide. Most of my friends have already graduated from college."

"It's not a judgment, Johanna, I'm just curious about your life at home," he said. He hoped he hadn't made her uncomfortable.

"Okay. Well, I work. I have an apartment. I used to have a roommate, but she went and got herself a boyfriend, so off she went. Yeesh." Jo laughed nervously, and her eyes darted around the pub.

"What do you do when you're not working or living alone in your apartment?" he teased.

"I hang out with my friends."

"Pubs?"

"Yeah, sure, sometimes. We do the usual stuff: go to movies, go to brunch sometimes. As you know, I love drawing, and I do all kinds of crafts. I've strong-armed my friends on occasion into those paint-and-wine classes."

Ian smiled. He was trying to picture her strong-arming anyone but couldn't see it. She was just too nice.

"What kind of crafts do you do?"

"I like anything that allows me to use my hands," she enthused. "I take those adult education courses at the high school every year. I've done pottery, painting, crocheting."

"And did you enjoy that?"

She nodded. "I do, really. There's a stained-glass course I'm going to take when I get home. I'm really looking forward to that."

Ian smiled. He pictured her wearing an artist's smock, bent over various pieces of colored glass, trying to make it all fit.

Ian lifted his pint and said, "Here's to stained glass!"

She clinked her glass against his. "Cheers."

They made general conversation, and Ian realized he was interested in what she had to say. When their pint glasses were drained, Jo stood, picked them up, and asked, "Ready for another?" He nodded, and she headed off in the direction of the bar.

Ian frowned when he saw the guy standing next to her at the bar lean down and whisper something to her.

"Ian!" someone shouted. Ian dragged his eyes away from Jo and turned in the direction of the voice. He smiled, but he was hesitant. It was two of his teammates, Donal and Brian. He hadn't seen them since he was in the hospital. Soon after the accident, they'd come to visit him, but it had been awkward because what does one say to an athlete when their career is cut short? As it turned out, not too much.

Pints in hand, they each pulled a chair from neighboring tables.

"Who are you here with?" Donal asked.

At that moment, Jo appeared and set their pint glasses on the table. Ian could tell by his teammates' expressions that they were confused but at the same time, found her attractive. It was hard not to.

Ian introduced Jo. The last thing he wanted was for them to get the impression that she was his carer or something.

"This is Johanna. Her nan and my nan are best friends. They're visiting from America."

With a thumb toward Ian, Donal teased, "How'd you get stuck with him? Doing penance or something?"

"Someone had to take a hit for the team," Jo teased, her laugh a light, silvery peal. Her eyes sparkled.

Donal and Brian's eyes widened, and they burst out laughing.

Ian had to pull his gaze away from her, as Brian was speaking to him.

"I think you've met your match, Ian," Brian said.

Ian couldn't help but wonder, had he?

They settled into a conversation about what was going on with the team. Donal and Brian brought Ian quickly up to speed. Ian felt a bit of anxiety over it; he missed it. More than anything. The manager had told him that there was a place for him in management, but Ian only wanted to play, which was why he hadn't returned any of his manager's phone calls or texts.

Ian kept his eye on Jo, mindful of trying to include her in the conversation. But she didn't know the first thing about rugby. A couple of times, he attempted to change the subject, but Donal and Brian continued to steer it back to the team. It wasn't only for Jo's sake he wanted a change in the conversation but for his own as well. It was hard to hear about the team moving on without him. But that's just what was happening—they had moved on.

Jo stood up and stepped out of the booth, laid her hand on Ian's shoulder, and whispered into his ear that she was going to the bathroom. Her hair fell forward and brushed the side of his neck. As she walked away, Ian was aware of other men in the pub giving her the once-over. His skin prickled. Was he jealous? Protective? And where had that come from?

"So what's going on between you and Jo?" Brian asked once Jo was out of earshot.

"What do you mean?" Ian asked. He drained the rest of his pint glass.

"I see the way you look at her and the way she looks at you, and I wondered if there was something there," Brian asked.

Ian shrugged, trying to appear casual. "Nothing. Like I said, she's a friend of the family. Are we ready for another round?"

"I'll get it," Donal said.

"Here, let me at least pay for it," Ian said. He didn't want to be dependent on anyone. He might not be able to play rugby, but he could still afford to buy a round or two. He removed his wallet from his back pocket, pulled a couple of notes from it, and slid them across the table to Donal, who didn't argue.

"Did I miss anything?" Jo asked as she reappeared, her eyes shining brightly. Her gaze bounced from Ian to his friends and then back to Ian again.

Ian smiled at her. "Not a thing, just ordering another round."

CHAPTER THIRTEEN

IT WAS GOOD TO see Ian smiling and laughing with his friends. Jo imagined this was how he used to be before his injury. His teammates looked genuinely happy to see him. She hoped it would be the first of many trips out of the house for Ian. It was important for him to rejoin society; he still had a lot to offer. He just needed to be convinced of that. Hopefully, this was the first step.

The pub was full of holiday cheer. A silver garland framed the mirror behind the bar. Alternating red and green ornaments hung from it. A gold-and-red banner reading "Happy Christmas" was strung across the breast of the fireplace in the corner.

Ian's friends were nice and funny. They recounted stories of their team's adventures playing at home and abroad. More than once, Jo smiled at Ian. Every story told indicated that when there was trouble or mischief to be had, Ian had been the ringleader. Feeling as if she might be an interloper, Jo spotted another booth empty out and thought she might head over there and give Ian some privacy with his friends. With her hand on the back of his chair, she leaned in and whispered that she was going to go sit in the other booth.

Ian surprised her by reaching out and taking hold of her hand. "Why?" His hand engulfed her smaller one, and Johanna felt her breath hitch in her throat. Her lips parted slightly, and she became aware of the hair standing up on her arm. He held on to her hand for a second longer than was necessary. Her heart fluttered.

"I thought you might want to be alone with your friends," she explained.

He gave a dismissive wave. "Not at all. Please, sit down, Johanna."

At one point she made her way up to the bar to get another round, although she had now switched to Coke. As she did, the fella who'd approached her earlier sidled up to her.

"You're back," he said with a laugh. He was short and wiry with a mop of dark hair that hung in his eyes.

"I am," she said and gave the bartender her order.

"I'm Chuck, by the way," he said, extending his hand.

Jo shook it. "I'm Jo."

"We don't get too many Yanks around here. Are you visiting family?"

"I'm with my grandmother; she left Ireland many years ago," Jo explained.

"Listen, can I take you out sometime?" he asked.

Jo's mouth fell open; she hadn't expected this. He seemed nice, but she wasn't interested.

"It's probably not a good idea," she said.

"Just one night," he said. "Dinner, drinks, dancing."

The bartender set a tray of drinks down on the bar, and Jo paid him.

"I appreciate the offer, but I'll have to refuse." She picked up the tray and said, "Nice meeting you, Chuck."

Never did she think she'd be asked out in Ireland. Even though she wasn't interested in Chuck, it kind of put a spring in her step as she made her way back to the table.

At midnight when the pub closed, Johanna and Ian spilled out onto the pavement with the rest of the revelers. It had stopped raining, and they made their way toward home. Halfway there, Johanna realized she'd left the umbrella behind at the pub.

"Leave it, Johanna. There's always an umbrella to be had in Ireland," he said.

Ian talked nonstop on the way home. Jo let him do the talking; she enjoyed seeing him so animated. She was relieved that grumpy wasn't his permanent state.

"You're quiet, everything all right?" he asked.

She grinned. "I didn't think I'd be able to get a word in edgewise." He laughed. She thought he should do that more often. Since she'd set foot in Ireland, she'd never seen him so relaxed.

"I saw that guy talking to you at the bar," Ian said.

Oh. There was a lot hanging there in the air.

"His name was Chuck," Jo said.

"He looked like he was chatting you up," Ian said.

"He did ask me out, but I said no," Jo explained.

"Why?" he asked.

"He wasn't my type."

"Interested in someone back in the States then?" he pressed.

Jo shrugged her shoulders. "No, but not because I'm not interested in meeting someone. It's just that I haven't met anyone I find interesting." Uncomfortable with the topic, she asked, "What about you? Girlfriend in the shadows?"

"No, I had a girlfriend, but once my career was over, she ended it," he said.

Jo cocked an eyebrow and regarded him for a moment. "Sounds like you dodged a bullet."

"I suppose so."

As his darkened house came into view, he said quietly, "I hate that house. It feels like a prison."

This confession startled her, and she sensed a curtain of doom beginning to descend. "Well, we'll have to do something about that." She nodded to herself as if this was the answer.

"Before the accident, I was never at home. Always on the go."

Johanna stopped walking. "Why should it be any different now, just because of a change in your circumstances?"

Ian stopped, shrugged, and looked back at his house. A slight mist fell around them as they stood there on the pavement.

"Ian?"

"I don't want to go out in public and have people staring at me, muttering, 'Oh, the poor creatur.'"

"The poor what?" she repeated. It had sounded like he'd said "crater."

"Yeah, 'poor creatur' is an Irish expression for someone you pity or have sympathy for," he explained, leaning on his crutches.

"But that didn't happen tonight. I saw people who were genuinely happy to see you. Besides, it's none of your business what other people think or say about you."

"What is that? Your thought for the day?" he asked, his black mood returning.

"Talk about the Dark Knight," she muttered sarcastically.

"Did you just call me the Dark Knight?" he asked.

Not knowing how he'd respond, she tilted her head and said, "Yes, I did."

"The Dark Knight as in Batman?" he asked.

"Yes."

He chuckled, which surprised her. They moved onto the footpath in front of Bridie's house. The Christmas lights that lined the gutter were still twinkling. The exterior light next to the front door cast a golden glow.

"So, you think I should still do what I can?" he asked.

"Yes, I do, and why don't we do these things while I'm here? You'd have some company," she said.

"And you don't mind driving?"

"Once I get used to it, I won't."

"What about tomorrow?" he asked.

Jo shook her head. "We're going to Gram's homeplace tomorrow. But I'm free the following day."

"Good, because first we'll continue with the driving lessons. Maybe go somewhere."

"That sounds like a good idea," Jo said, hoping he wouldn't change his mind.

He took a step closer and lowered his voice. "So, Johanna Mueller thinks I shouldn't let this injury interfere with my life. That I should just get on with it."

"Yes."

In the pale light, Ian's eyes sparkled, and one corner of his mouth lifted in a grin.

"We'll go see the country then?" When she nodded, he added with a lifted eyebrow, "There's no boyfriend back home that's going to come gunning for me?"

Jo laughed. "No."

His eyes locked with hers. "Right then." He leaned into her and seemed to be considering something. Jo's lips parted slightly in anticipation. If he was going to kiss her, she was all for it. But he took a step back and gave her a small smile.

"Go on inside now before you catch a chill," he said.

Jo unlocked the front door, aware that Ian's eyes were on her. Without a word, he nodded toward her, turned away, and headed up the footpath toward his home. Jo closed the door softly behind her, wishing he had kissed her good-night.

In the morning, Jo went off with Gram and Bridie to visit Gram's homeplace. Bridie had prepared a big Irish fry-up for breakfast and afterward, Jo and Gram insisted on doing the washup.

Gram's homeplace was twenty minutes away. Jo climbed into the back seat of Bridie's car and fought the urge to doze off. She'd barely slept at all the previous night, her mind entrenched in a constant replay of the pleasant evening she'd spent with Ian. She was pretty sure he'd been about to kiss her at the end of the night. But then suddenly, he'd changed his mind.

Gram could not hide her excitement at visiting her childhood home. Jo had seen pictures of it over the years, but nothing would beat seeing it in person. As Gram and Bridie chatted and laughed nonstop in the front seat, Jo leaned against the window in the back and revisited every interaction with Ian many times.

The sun shone. Despite it being December, the grass looked green, and big, fluffy white clouds dotted the bright blue sky. Jo watched the scenery whizz by the window, never tiring of the endless pastures of cows.

The plan was to visit the homeplace and then to visit Bridie's brother, Tom, on the neighboring farm, where Bridie had grown up. He and his wife, Nora, had invited the three of them for luncheon.

As they pulled up to the farm, Gram went quiet. Bridie parked along the edge of the grass, and the three of them exited the car.

Jo stood next to her grandmother on the side of the rural country road, the ruins of her childhood home before them. It was a traditional Irish farmhouse with a door and three windows at the front and three windows at the back. There were no windows on the gable ends of the home. The walls, a faded apricot, were covered in moss and lichen. The front door had once been painted brown, but it was now chipped and peeling. The roof had caved in a long time ago, but two chimney breasts still stood.

Jo helped her grandmother traverse the overgrown grass until they were standing in front of the house.

"Oh, it's such a pity, the state of it!" Gram wailed.

Jo reached out and squeezed her hand.

"I wish we could have kept it." Gram's eyes filled with tears.

"There's houses like this all over the country," Bridie said behind them.

"Which room was yours, Gram?" Jo asked.

"This one right here." Gram pointed to the window on the far right.

Jo stepped forward and peered in the window. The small room held a fireplace and a brass bedframe, and a wooden wardrobe stood in the corner. Gram stepped up next to Jo and peeked inside.

"You had a fireplace in your room?" Jo asked, incredulous.

"Yes, all the rooms had them. Back in those days, there was no such thing as central heating."

"And the toilet was on the outside of the house," Bridie said behind them.

"Oh my goodness, that's my bed. Why didn't they take the furniture out of the house? It would still have been usable," Gram lamented. "What a waste."

Jo didn't have an answer for her. She stepped away and moved to the middle window.

"What room was this?"

"That's the sitting room, where my mother did her entertaining." Gram stood alongside Jo, and they peered in the window. The panes were long gone, and Jo could see debris scattered across the floor. There was a framed picture of Jesus and the Blessed Mother, the glass broken and the picture yellowed and warped. Wallpaper hung off in strips, and the fireplace had garbage in it. It was sad that her grandmother had to see her childhood home in this condition.

They went on to the next window, which looked into what used to be the kitchen. This room housed a large hearth and a small wooden table that had once been painted a pale blue but was now blackened and chipped due to its age and exposure to inclement weather.

"Why don't I get a picture of the two of you in front of the house?" Bridie asked.

"That's a great idea," Jo said, pulling her phone out of her pocket. She set up the camera and handed it to Bridie, showing her which button to press. She took her place next to Gram and put her arm around her shoulder. Gram was quiet, and Jo was sure she was overcome with emotion; she knew she would be if it were her.

After Bridie took a few snaps, Gram went back to looking at her old home. "If these walls could talk, boy, the stories they would tell."

Jo smiled, picturing the generations coming and going through all the seasons here in the family home. She was grateful she'd gotten the chance to see it. Her gaze landed on the gently rolling hills and pastures of green and gold behind the house.

"I don't see how people could leave Ireland," Jo observed. "The scenery is so beautiful."

"You can't eat the scenery," Bridie quipped behind her.

As Gram looked around, took it all in, and reflected, Jo pulled her sketch pad out of her bag. She leaned against Bridie's car, set her pencils out on the hood, and began sketching.

"I'm ready," Gram announced after a half hour. "I'd like to go to the cemetery next, to visit the graves of my parents and brother."

Jo had drawn a rough sketch. Quickly, she took photos of the place at many different angles so she could finish the drawing later.

"Jo, do you need more time?" Gram asked.

"Nope."

The church and its accompanying graveyard were a three-minute drive from the old homeplace. Jo climbed out of the back seat and took in the sights of the graveyard. In the middle of the cemetery stood the ruins of a long-abandoned church, two walls and a roof missing. The remaining walls had been reclaimed by the grass and ivy. The newer church next to the cemetery was a small gray stone building with an asphalt drive lined with towering oaks, their limbs now bare. It had a desolate feeling.

They stopped at the graves of Gram's family members, and then they made the rounds through the cemetery, including a stop at the grave of Bridie's parents.

"A cuppa would be just grand right about now," Bridie said as they walked out of the graveyard. She looped her arm through Gram's. "Let's see what Nora has for us."

Chapter Fourteen

I T WAS POURING RAIN in the morning, and the sky was the color of charcoal. Ian rolled over and pulled the blanket over his head. He'd promised Jo that they would go out for a driving lesson and maybe go somewhere. What had made him do that? His booze-fueled good mood at the end of the night in the pub, that's what. In the harsh light of day, he no longer felt the good humor that had intoxicated him two nights ago. With Jo and the two grans gone all day the day before, he had done nothing but think about Jo.

He'd almost kissed her. Almost. It had seemed, in the moment, like the most natural thing to do. The thought had been impulsive. And these days, he couldn't afford that. But that didn't mean he didn't wonder what her lips would feel like. What she would taste like.

He folded his hands behind his head and stared at the ceiling, sighing. He knew the pattern of the ceiling by heart. From the small water stain in the corner to the hairline crack that ran the width of it. Staring at it had allowed him to do a lot of thinking.

That night in the pub, he'd felt something he hadn't felt in a long time: *normal.* He'd been just a guy out with a girl and his mates. You couldn't get any more normal than that. But surely, that had been nothing but a blip.

He heard a knock at his front door and he groaned. If anything, Jo was persistent. He had promised her that they'd do something. Best to see it through. And as much as he hated to admit it, he was looking forward to seeing her. He sat up and grabbed his crutches.

By the time he reached the door, there was a second knock.

Jo stood on his doorstep, wearing a brown suede jacket over a navy turtleneck and a pair of jeans.

"Ian, good morning!"

"Come on in," Ian said, holding the door open for her.

There was some hesitation on Jo's part as she looked him over. "Did you not want to go driving this morning?"

Ian rubbed the back of his head. "I'm running late, that's all. Can you give me ten minutes?"

"Sure, take your time," she said.

"Fix yourself a cup of tea if you want," he said over his shoulder.

"No, thank you, I drank enough tea at your grandmother's house this morning. I could float a cruise liner."

Ian chuckled. Maybe Nana was right about this being a good thing for him. He decided he liked company. *Her* company.

It took him less than ten minutes to wash his face, brush his teeth, and get dressed. He found Jo parked on the sofa.

"Your grandmother said we're to be back by two. She's making a roasted chicken," Jo informed him.

"Two and not one?"

Jo shook her head. "No, she and Gram had a long day yesterday, and they were late getting up."

"All right." Ian nodded. "Let's go."

"Did you want to eat breakfast or something?" she asked.

What he wanted was not to hold her up. He should have been ready when she'd arrived. He really needed to start pulling himself together.

Once they were situated in the car, Jo paused for a moment and reacquainted herself with the setup.

"All right, remember what I told you? About the clutch? First, second, third gear, and so on and so forth?" he asked.

"Which gears are so on and so forth?" she asked with a straight face.

Despite himself, Ian laughed. "All right, Johanna, let's go."

Jo started the car and attempted to put it in first, but her timing was off, resulting in an awful grinding noise.

Ian winced. "You're not going to start grinding gears now, are you?"

After a few rough starts, she managed to get the car out of first and into second. Ian directed her to drive away from the town, toward the country. Once she was in fourth gear, the ride was smooth. It was just getting going that she seemed to have trouble with. But that would come. Hopefully, sooner rather than later. He didn't know how much more his car could take.

As she drove, she leaned forward in the seat with her white-knuckled hands gripping the steering wheel.

"How does your family celebrate Christmas in America?" he asked.

Jo looked quickly over at him. "Ian, I can't talk right now, I'm trying to concentrate on my driving." She returned her attention to the road.

Ian bit his lip to suppress a grin.

After half an hour, Ian glanced at his watch and decided they had time for a quick detour.

He looked over at Jo, an idea forming in his head, thinking she might be a good sport.

"Johanna, do you mind if we stop and see a relative of mine?"

Some unnamed emotion played across her face. *Yeah, this is going to be fun*, Ian thought.

"A relative?" she repeated, her brow furrowing. She didn't take her eyes off the road.

Ian nodded. "He's a far-out relation. A distant cousin. I always stop by whenever I'm in this area."

Jo bit her lip. "He won't mind us dropping in without calling first?" Her expression was skeptical.

"Nah, he doesn't have a phone."

Her eyes widened. "He doesn't have a phone? In this day and age?" she asked, incredulous.

Ian shook his head. "There are still a few old-timers in the country who live in houses with no electricity or running water."

"Wow. So he's an old-timer?" Jo asked.

"Kind of," Ian said, staring out the window.

"Should we stop and pick something up? Maybe a cake or something?" Jo rambled more to herself than to him. "I'd hate to drop in unannounced and empty-handed." She thought for a moment and said, "What about flowers or a poinsettia? I mean, it is Christmastime."

Ian smiled. "A poinsettia would be lovely. He'd really appreciate that."

He pointed to a gas station up ahead. "Pull into that petrol station there. They've got a shop as well. We'll be able to get a poinsettia there."

"Okay."

She pulled in and may have skipped a few gears getting back to first. Once the car was parked, he reminded her to put on the emergency brake.

"Huh, I never think about that."

"It will come with time," he reassured her. He leaned over toward her so he could pull his wallet out of his back pocket. She smelled nice and he tried not to groan. He took a twenty-euro note out of his leather wallet and handed it to her. "Here, get whatever you want."

Jo shook her head. "I got this."

He felt a surge of frustration. There wasn't a lot he could do with a pretty girl. He couldn't take her out dancing or hold her hand as they walked along the footpath. He couldn't drive her wherever she wanted to go. But he could pay for things. That much he could do. That much he wanted to do.

He shoved the bill toward her. "Please, Johanna."

Sensing his annoyance, she took the note and said quietly, "Okay."

She jumped out of the car and walked toward the entrance of the petrol station. He liked how she had a little bounce to her step, but her head was down. He sighed. Why did he have to let his bad humor ruin everything? Here she was, driving him all around when she could have hopped on a tour bus and seen Ireland herself. He steeled himself to be nicer and to not be offended by everything she suggested.

Ten minutes later, Jo came bouncing out of the shop with a poinsettia in one hand and a distinctive rectangular red cookie tin labeled *Jacob's Afternoon Tea.* Ian smiled to himself. The girl had spirit, he had to give her that.

She was talking before she opened the door, and her voice filled the car like bubbles being blown from a wand.

"I saw these and I couldn't resist," she said, showing him the tin. "There were all these cute boxes and tins of cookies! Really, I had a hard time choosing." She reached around to the back seat and laid the tin and the poinsettia on the floor.

"You chose well, these are my favorite," Ian said. "They only come out at Christmas."

"That makes sense," she agreed, buckling her seat belt. "Christmas is a time to make cookies."

"We don't really make biscuits here for Christmas," Ian said. "It's all about mince pies, Christmas cakes, and puddings."

"I've had the mince pies. They're delicious," she said.

Ian laughed. "They are."

"Anyway, I thought when we visit your cousin, we could have a cup of tea and a 'biscuit,' as you call it," she said.

Ian suppressed a grin. "That's thoughtful of you."

She started the car and with a shrieking noise from the grinding gears, they were off.

"Where are we going?" she asked.

"Wexford town. He's right in the town center."

Jo made a moue of distaste. "I have to drive through a town center?"

"No worries, you'll be grand."

Ian gave her directions to Wexford town. He could hardly wait, wanting to see how this all played out.

When they arrived in the town center, Ian instructed, "There's a parking spot there, right in front of the bookie's, next to that barber shop. My relative is just around the corner."

"Are you sure this is a good idea?" Jo asked as she pulled in to the spot and parked.

Ian nodded. "Oh sure. I always stop whenever I'm in Wexford town, you know, to pay my respects."

That seemed to appease Jo, and they got out of the car.

"It'll be a flying visit," Ian said.

Jo frowned. "Wouldn't that be kind of rude, to not sit down and chat?"

Ian tilted his head. "He's not much for the chat. Let's go, you'll see for yourself."

Ian removed his crutches from the back seat as Jo retrieved the poinsettia and the tin of cookies.

They walked toward the end of the street.

"This is a nice little town," Jo said, looking around.

At the corner, next to a bike shop painted in bright blue, Ian paused. Jo stopped talking and followed his line of sight.

Ian had come to rest at a statue depicting an athlete in motion, gripping a hurley—Nicky Rackard, who'd played for Wexford in the 1940s and '50s and was considered by some to be one of Ireland's greatest hurlers of all time.

Ian watched the expression on Jo's face transform from unreadable to confused and smiled to himself.

Jo stood beside him, staring at the statue. A frown etched her forehead. "What's this?"

"Johanna, I'd like you to meet Nicky Rackard, a relative of mine," Ian said.

Jo blinked, and her gaze bounced from the statue back to Ian and then came to rest on the statue again. Then she burst out laughing. Ian grinned. He knew she'd be a good sport about it.

A grin spread across her face. "A relative, huh?"

Ian nodded. "His grandmother and Nana's grandmother were like third or fourth cousins. Far out, of course."

"Of course," she said with a smile.

She laughed again, and Ian couldn't help but join in. You could say a lot of things about Johanna. But one thing you couldn't say was that she lacked a sense of humor.

Once she recovered, she put the poinsettia in front of the statue on top of the concrete block. The vibrant red stood in contrast to the dark statue.

"Merry Christmas, Nicky," she said.

She removed the plastic seal from the package of Afternoon Tea, pulled off the lid, and held out the tin to Ian. He chose a chocolate-covered digestive. Jo picked a red-foiled biscuit before replacing the lid and placing the tin on the ground.

She unwrapped her cookie and took a bite of it, staring at the statue. There was nothing about her that was unappealing, Ian thought to himself. The bright eyes, the reddish hair, the clear complexion. He liked spending time with her. It made him forget his troubles.

Jo turned back to Ian, held up her biscuit, and asked, "Now aren't you glad we didn't come empty-handed?"

They arrived back at the house with only minutes to spare. As soon as they walked through Nana's front door, they were greeted with the smell of roast chicken. Ian's stomach growled in response. Roasted chicken was one of his favorite meals, especially when Nana cooked it.

From the kitchen came giggling.

Jo laughed. "Oh, those two, that's all they do is laugh at everything."

"Nana likes the craic," Ian said. He knew for a fact that his grandmother had been so looking forward to Mary's visit that it was all she had talked about.

The two of them went through to the kitchen and as soon as they entered, their grandmothers burst out laughing.

With a grin, Ian shook his head. "I don't know about these two. I think they've been nipping at the sherry."

Jo nodded, laughing. "We should breathalyze them before they make the gravy."

"Lumpy gravy wouldn't do," he said. He and Jo looked at each other, and their eyes locked. There was merriment in Jo's expression. Ian couldn't help but smile.

Chapter Fifteen

J O SET THE TABLE while Gram and Nana went about serving up the dinner. Ian managed to carry over a water pitcher and then the butter dish. As Jo laid down the place settings, she kept stealing glances at him.

She liked this side of him. She wished she could have known him before his injury. She'd bet he was a lot of fun to hang around with. After the night at the pub and then this morning, she felt encouraged. She liked the way she felt when she was with him.

As they all sat down together, she noticed her plate was heaping with tender slices of chicken, mashed potatoes and gravy, a sage-and-onion stuffing, a carrot-and-parsnip mash, turnip, and broccoli. If she finished all this, she wouldn't have to eat for a week.

Scruff circled around Ian's chair and finally came to rest on the floor next to it, his head raised, his gaze fixed on Ian.

"Ian, do not feed the dog from the table," Bridie said.

"No, Nana, I won't," Ian said, but he whispered to the dog, "I'll save you some chicken."

"Where did the two of you head off to this morning?" Bridie asked.

"We went for a drive to Wexford town," Jo said.

"That must have been nice," Bridie said absentmindedly as she poured liberal amounts of gravy over her own plate of food.

"It was," Jo said truthfully.

Ian shrugged, not taking his eyes off of his plate. He scooped up a forkful of mashed potatoes. "Johanna's starting to get the hang of driving a manual."

He didn't say anything about stopping to see his "relative," and Jo decided she wouldn't say anything either. It was kind of nice to keep between them, she thought, almost like a private joke.

Bridie recounted to Ian their visit to Mary's homeplace, and the spread laid out at her brother's and his wife's home.

"The food! You know how Nora is, Ian," Bridie said. "If you go away from Nora's table hungry, it's your own fault."

"How are Tom and Nora?" Ian asked.

"They're well. Tom's walking great since he had his hip replaced," Bridie informed him. "They asked after you. You should really visit them once you're driving again."

"I will. I like visiting relatives," Ian said. He glanced sideways at Jo and winked.

Jo pressed her lips together to suppress a grin.

"What kind of trouble have you and Mary been getting into?" Ian asked his grandmother. This question resulted in a round of giggles and laughter between the two elderly women. He grinned. "That much?"

"We've been having a ball," Gram said, wiping a tear from her eye. She and Nana started laughing again.

Jo said, "I don't know who is the bad influence here."

Ian regarded their grandmothers and pronounced, "It looks to be pretty even."

Once the dinner plates were cleared, Nana and Gram served up dessert.

Jo leaned back in her chair and folded her arms across her abdomen. She blew out a breath, and her bangs lifted off her face. "I don't know if I can. I'm pretty stuffed." She'd been hungrier than she thought.

But a plate was put in front of her with a mini mince pie on it.

"Try one of those," Gram said with a nod toward the floral dessert plate. "Bridie and I made those last night."

Bridie stood at the counter, using an electric whisk to whip up a bowl of cream. "You can't have Christmas without mince pies."

"How many for you, Ian?" Gram asked.

"Two is good," he said.

As Nana doled out a generous dollop of cream on top of their mince pies, Jo asked, "What kind of plans do you have for the rest of the day?"

"We're going into the city to see a pantomime."

"By yourselves?" Ian asked.

Nana shook her head. "No, we're going with the retirement group. The bus pulls away from the church at six sharp."

"What about you two?" Gram asked. "Any plans for the afternoon?"

Both Gram and Nana stopped what they were doing and looked expectantly at Jo and Ian. Jo felt like it was a test she must pass.

"We'll figure something out," Ian said smoothly. "I'll take Johanna to see something."

Out of the corner of her eye, Jo regarded him. He sat so close to her that his arm practically brushed against hers. She studied that arm as unobtrusively as possible, the ropey veins running the length of it. She would have liked to reach out and trace a finger along those veins, imagining how hard they would feel beneath her fingertips.

Deciding she couldn't go down that road, no matter how much she wanted to, she reminded herself that he used to be a professional rugby player. He was a celebrity in his own right, and celebrities didn't usually choose girls who sold clothes at the mall.

Jo tried to focus her attention on her mince pie, which was yummy. Gram had made mince pies at Christmas for as long as Jo could remember. Nana was right; it wasn't Christmas without them.

But she found herself wondering what type of girl Ian had dated in the past. Most likely a looker, she concluded. The image of a leggy blonde with her arm looped through Ian's came to mind, and Jo tried not to let it depress her.

After dinner, Jo offered to do the cleanup.

"Do you mind?" Nana asked. "It's just that there's a repeat episode of one of the *Mrs. Brown's Boys* Christmas specials on RTE this afternoon, and I thought Mary might enjoy it."

"We can watch that before we go to the pantomime," Gram chirped.

"That's what I thought too."

"I don't mind at all," Jo said honestly. Bridie and Gram had gone to the trouble of making a beautiful dinner; they'd certainly earned the right to put their feet up.

As they headed out of the kitchen, Bridie said to Ian, "You'll help Jo, won't you, Ian?"

By her tone and pointed look, she made it clear that it was more of a command than a question.

Ian simply nodded his head and grabbed his crutches. Once standing, he hobbled over to the sink.

"Maybe I could bring the plates over and you could load them," Jo suggested.

"Sure, that's fine," he said. "Just save a bit of the chicken for the dog."

Jo nodded, putting aside some chicken scraps on a separate plate. She brought over the rest of the plates, scraped them off into the bin, and handed them to Ian, who loaded them into the dishwasher. They worked in tandem, wordlessly, focusing on their task. As Ian poured dishwasher soap into the compartment and turned it on, Jo wiped down the table and the countertops.

Ian put some chicken into the dog's dish and Scruff gobbled it up, his tail wagging.

When they were finished, they glanced around the tidy kitchen. From the front of the house came the sound of laughter and a television soundtrack. Both Ian and Jo smiled.

Ian glanced at his watch. "It's still early, will we do something? Take a drive?"

Jo was nodding before he finished his sentence. "Yeah, sure."

Jo felt her driving was coming along; she only ground the gears twice. Ian must be getting used to it, she thought; he'd refrained from commenting and only raised an eyebrow once.

They ended up heading back to Wexford town, to the ruins of Selskar Abbey, which dated back to the twelfth century. For a Sunday afternoon, it wasn't that crowded. Finally, there was a little bit of sun, and the green grass glittered beneath it. Ian trailed along on his crutches as they made their way around the impressive grounds.

Jo admired the red sandstone walls on the eastern side. She marveled at all of it. Everything was so *old*.

"I'll have to come back one day soon with my sketchbook," she said.

"You seem passionate about sketching," Ian said.

Jo nodded, shielding her eyes from the bright sunshine. She'd never thought to bring her sunglasses with her.

"I am, I love it."

"Did you ever think about making a career out of it?"

"A starving artist? No, thanks."

Ian stopped and leaned on his crutches. "Who said you had to be starving?"

Jo shrugged.

"There must be something you could do with an art degree to support yourself."

"I don't know."

"Have you ever thought of looking into it?" he asked, walking on.

"No, I guess I've boxed myself into thinking that there wouldn't be a lot of career opportunities," Jo admitted, biting her lip.

"Do you need to sketch or draw every day?"

"Yes," she said. "It's almost like breathing. I find it relaxes me."

"Do what you love, Johanna. Life's too short to be stuck in a job you're miserable at."

"Did you feel the same way about rugby?" Jo asked, hoping he wouldn't find her question intrusive.

"I did. I've been playing for as long as I can remember. I used to eat, breathe, and sleep rugby. Playing for the Irish Rovers was a lifelong dream."

They walked on in silence. After a bit, Jo said, "What will you do, going forward?"

A bitter laugh escaped Ian. "That's just it. I don't know."

"You couldn't work in some capacity with your team?" she ventured.

Ian shook his head before Jo even had the whole sentence out of her mouth.

"If I can't play rugby, I don't want to be on the sidelines watching everyone else play."

"Jeez, that kind of thinking is self-limiting, isn't it?"

"Maybe it is, but it's how I feel," he said.

Jo had nothing to add so kept quiet.

Ian changed the subject. "Will we go for some tea?"

"That would be lovely."

They made their way to the tea shop, and there was no more talk about careers in art or playing rugby. They kept it general, and the time flew.

CHAPTER SIXTEEN

WHEN THEY PULLED UP to Ian's house, it was beginning to get dark. There were no lights on at Bridie's, as she and Gram had left for the pantomime and wouldn't be home until late.

They got out of the car, and Ian glanced at Bridie's darkened house.

"Why don't you come on over? I'm sure we could find something to do—er, watch on the telly," Ian said. He didn't know why, but he wasn't ready to part company with Jo yet.

"You're not too tired?" Jo asked.

Ian bristled. "I'm not eighty, Johanna."

"Okay, but I won't stay long."

"You can stay as long as you like," he said.

Once inside, he asked, "Did you want a cup of tea or something to eat?"

She shook her head. "I couldn't eat another thing."

He nodded. "Make yourself at home."

They removed their coats, but they'd hardly gotten settled in the sitting room before there was a knock at the front door.

Ian answered it and his smile disappeared. He couldn't hide his surprise. It was Kevin Breen, the coach of his rugby club. Kevin had come up to visit him in the hospital and had tried to contact him numerous times since.

"Come on in, Kevin," Ian said tightly.

"You weren't answering my calls or texts, so I thought I'd stop in and wish you a Happy Christmas in person," Kevin said.

"Thanks, I appreciate that," Ian said, leading him toward the sitting room. "Have a seat."

When the man spotted Jo, he said, "I'm sorry, Ian, I didn't know you had company."

"Maybe I should get going," Jo interrupted.

"Not necessary." Ian introduced them. "Kevin, this is my friend Johanna. Johanna, this is Kevin Breen, coach of the Irish Rovers."

"Nice to meet you," Jo said, shaking his hand.

He nodded. "I'm not staying long," Kevin said. He held up a tin of Afternoon Tea biscuits and another, circular in shape, labeled *Cadbury Roses.*

"Thanks," Ian said. His coach set the tins on the coffee table and sat in the armchair across from Jo.

Ian offered him some tea.

"As I said, I'm not staying long," Kevin said. "You seem to be doing well."

Ian was about to protest, but he saw his coach's gaze drift toward Johanna and then land back at him. He'd been spending so much time with Jo; had he not noticed that he was starting to move on? Emerging from his dark abyss? If he was, he had Jo to thank for it.

"Just taking it one day at a time," Ian said.

"That's all any of us can do," Kevin replied.

There was a moment of awkward silence.

"The invites have been sent out for the Christmas banquet this weekend, but they haven't received your RSVP yet," Kevin said.

"I'll probably give it a miss this year," Ian said. He used to love the annual Christmas party. A night to dress up, enjoy good food and drink, do a lot of dancing, and then go pub-crawling afterward with his date, his teammates, and their girlfriends.

But Kevin wouldn't take no for an answer. "You know it'll be a good time, and your teammates would really like to see you."

"Look, Kevin, I really appreciate it, but I don't think so," Ian said. He'd never missed the Christmas banquet, and every year he'd had a different girl on his arm. But not this year. It wouldn't be the same: no dancing, and he didn't think he could take the looks of pity from his former teammates. No, this year, it would be a quiet night in.

His coach sighed. "The team misses you. You were an integral part of it."

"That's when I played on the team. That part of my life is over," Ian said, trying to keep the bitterness out of his voice. He'd had a pretty good day with Jo. The first one in a long time. He didn't want grief over his old life casting a pall over the day. Or ruining it.

"There are other things in the organization you can do without actually playing on the field."

Ian said nothing. Jo remained on the sofa, quiet.

"I'll leave these with you," the coach said, rising from his chair and with a glance at Johanna he dropped two tickets to the banquet on the coffee table.

"Thanks," Ian said.

He followed Kevin to the door.

"Just think about it, Ian. You can't hide out here forever." Kevin paused. "Your girl might enjoy a night out."

Ian didn't bother correcting him or disabusing him of the notion that Johanna was his girlfriend. He could only wish. She was young and pretty and certainly wouldn't be interested in a washed-up sports star. He said good night to his former coach and closed the door behind him.

"Do you mind if I open these?" Jo asked, holding up the tin of Roses.

Ian couldn't help but smile. "Not at all."

After studying the legend on the bottom of the tin, which turned out to be filled with individually wrapped chocolate candies, Jo peeled off the clear cellophane, opened the lid, and chose two candies, one in an orange wrapper and the other in a pink one. "Hmm, Tangy Orange Creme and Strawberry Dream."

"I suppose you think I should go to this banquet?" Ian set his crutches against the arm of the sofa and sat down next to Jo.

Jo shrugged and popped a piece of candy into her mouth. "It's up to you, Ian. I can't make that decision for you."

Ian sighed.

Jo nodded toward the tin of candy. "Did you want one?"

He shook his head.

"What kind of Christmas party is it?" Jo asked.

"You know, the usual. Everyone gets dressed up, and it's at some nice hotel where there's a lot of food, drink, and dancing."

Jo's mouth opened slightly. "That sounds wonderful."

"You probably do the same where you work?"

Jo snorted. "Not on your life. Our Christmas party used to consist of going to lunch at a local restaurant, separate checks. And for the last two years, I was scheduled to work, so I couldn't go."

He didn't miss the disappointment in her voice. A thought occurred to him.

"If I were to go to this Christmas party, would you go with me?" he asked. He averted his gaze, afraid to read the reaction on her face. What was wrong with him that he was putting himself through what would obviously be a rejection? He didn't have to wait too long.

"I'd love to go," she said quietly.

His head snapped up. "You would?"

"Yes," she said. "I would. Seriously. This is formal dress?"

Ian nodded. "Suits and frocks."

She helped herself to another piece of candy. "I'd look forward to it."

"It's a banquet. Dinner. Then awards are handed out and there's a lot of speeches. It might be boring. I wouldn't be able to do any dancing."

"That's okay by me, dancing isn't one of my strong points. Besides, I'd be more interested in the food. Is it good?"

Ian laughed, loving her honesty. "Usually."

"Okay."

Ian didn't know what to say.

Jo said, "I should get going. Thanks for today, Ian."

Ian held out his hand, palm up, and said, "No, thank you, Johanna. It was great to get out of the house."

Her smile was brighter than all the Christmas lights combined.

"I really should get going," she repeated, standing up.

He could only nod.

As he walked her to the door, he asked, "What are your plans for tomorrow?"

Jo shrugged. "I don't know yet. I was thinking of taking a bus to Dublin to visit the National Gallery of Ireland."

He knew he couldn't monopolize all her time. Something unsaid was left hanging in the air.

"Why don't you grab your bus to Dublin in the morning, go to your museum, and then maybe we could do something on Friday," he suggested casually. He didn't want to appear overeager—or worse, desperate—even though that's how he felt.

Her smile brightened. "That sounds like a plan. Where will we go?"

Ian grinned. "It's a surprise, but it's an atypical tourist attraction."

"Oh, I like it!" she said.

He laughed, and she surprised him when she stood on her tiptoes to kiss him on the cheek. "Good night, Ian."

"Good night, Johanna."

Chapter Seventeen

On Friday, Jo met Ian outside at eight in the morning. He'd left a message for her at Bridie's the day before while she was away in Dublin. Bridie and Gram were all atwitter at these recent developments—namely, Ian leaving his house. And *wanting* to. Bridie had revisited the idea of Jo being paid for her time, but Jo wouldn't hear of it, and Gram had backed her up.

Although the day dawned bright and sunny, it was damp, and Jo had bundled up in a hat, coat, scarf, and gloves.

"Ready?" Ian asked.

Jo nodded and followed him to his car, where he handed her the keys.

As Jo buckled up, she asked, "Where are we going today?" She wondered what ruin, castle or "relative" he would show her. He could take her to the inside of his grandmother's garden shed, and she was pretty sure she'd love that too.

Ian's grin was mischievous. "We're going to a sanctuary."

"Birds? Butterflies?"

Ian laughed and shook his head. "Close. Donkeys."

"How is that close?" Jo asked. "There's a sanctuary for don-keys?"

Ian nodded. "It's been here for decades. Since the eighties, I think."

"Huh. Who knew there'd be a need for a donkey sanctuary." Jo turned this over in her mind, thinking that she would, indeed, like to see this place. There was certainly nothing like that back home.

They drove through hilly green pastures, watching the sun make its ascent in the east.

"How was Dublin?" Ian asked.

"Wonderful, I loved it," she replied.

"It is a great city," Ian concurred. "What did you do there?"

She told him how she'd spent the majority of the day at the National Gallery of Ireland and then bought a ticket for a hop-on hop-off bus.

"It's the perfect way to see a city," Jo said. "You get off at each stop, go look at everything, get back on, and go to the next stop."

"Did you enjoy the National Gallery?"

"It was amazing! Their collection is sublime," Jo gushed.

"Did you have a favorite piece?" he asked.

Jo didn't have to think about it. "*The Meeting on the Turret Stairs*, without a doubt." Jo could still feel the anguish the painting depicted. Two medieval lovers, about to be parted, saying goodbye. The contrast of the woman's royal blue dress with the long red braid hanging down her back had stuck with Jo. But it was the way the man—dressed in a chain-mail shirt and hood—lovingly held her arm, laying a kiss on it, that had made her heart ache.

"That's a famous one. It was voted Ireland's favorite paint-ing," Ian said.

"It's easy to see why."

Jo thought more about all the emotion the painting portrayed and felt she understood how the couple in the painting felt. To be in love and to be separated.

"What are you thinking about? You've got a dreamy look on your face," Ian said.

"Have I?"

Jo noticed that he hung on to the grab handle above the passenger-side window. Did he not know what to do with his hand, or was it a lack of confidence in her driving? Deciding it was the latter, she slowed down.

After a few minutes, Ian spoke. "Is there a reason you're driving so slow? I mean, there's no one else on the road."

"I thought I might be going too fast."

"For who?"

She shrugged.

They were taking some backroads to a village named Liscarroll in County Cork, where the sanctuary was located. Jo tried not to be distracted by the lovely scenery out the window, but it was proving to be just about impossible. She wanted to see everything. It was so beautiful. No two houses or farms were alike. Sometimes, the fields and pastures seemed to go on forever. Other times, you couldn't see through the dense blackthorn hedges. And the pattern was the same: drive through a small village that usually had a few buildings like a post office, church, and a shop, then through countryside, and then through another village. Crossroads and T-junctions were signposted with bright-green signs with reflective white writing. Jo liked the way the Gaelic name appeared at the top with the English name on the bottom. Halfway there, she realized she didn't really need a GPS. She found it was pretty straightforward; all she had to do was follow the signposts marked "Mallow," and from there she followed the signposts that read "Liscarroll."

She was amazed at the number of ruins across the countryside.

"Nothing gets torn down in the country," she marveled as they passed the ruin of another farmhouse with its roof caved in and windows broken. The door flapped open in the breeze. Gram's homeplace came to mind.

"Nah, I guess it doesn't. See the newer-build house next to it?" Ian asked with a nod toward the structure about ten yards from the ruin of the older house.

"Yes."

"It's probably still the same family that built the newer house. They just carried their belongings from the old place to the new one."

"Well, smart on them," Jo observed. "They didn't have to walk far."

Ian laughed. "No, they did not."

They drove the rest of the short journey in companionable silence. Jo noticed the sign for the donkey sanctuary and made the turn.

They parked and headed to the admission. There was no fee, but the sanctuary was receptive to donations, as it was a charitable organization. Jo and Ian threw money into the collection box.

"Who knew that donkeys needed to be rescued," Jo mused as they walked through.

"There are a lot of donkeys in Ireland and unfortunately, they get abandoned or neglected."

The expansive outdoor space featured a grassy paddock with timber fencing, two slats each. There were a lot of donkeys, and some regarded them with curiosity. A few walked over to the fence and either stuck their heads through the two wood slats or over the top.

"Gosh, aren't they cute," Jo said.

"They're very social animals," Ian said, "but they do have a mean kick. So don't ever stand behind them."

Jo didn't think she'd ever have another opportunity to be near a donkey, never mind behind one. There certainly wasn't a plethora of them around at home.

Ian looked at her as if sensing her doubt. "Seriously. An uncle of mine was kicked in the head by a donkey. He hasn't been right since."

"What happened to him?"

"He died."

It wasn't funny but it was. Jo suppressed a grin.

"Are we allowed to pet them?" she asked.

Ian nodded. "Sure, go ahead."

Tentatively, Jo reached out her hand, then pulled it back and tried again. The donkey nearest her waited patiently for her to make up her mind. Jo laughed and finally petted the creature.

"Oh, you're a gorgeous girl," Jo said.

The donkey's ears flattened.

"It's a boy," Ian informed her.

"How do you know?" Jo asked. Ian grinned and Jo blushed. "Never mind."

Chapter Eighteen

After the donkey sanctuary and a brief visit to another castle ruin in Liscarroll, they got back in the car and headed further south through County Cork toward the fishing village of Kinsale. They spent the rest of the day there, exploring the seaside town.

They stopped at Charles Fort, a star-shaped fortress located on the Atlantic, which had been completed in the seventeenth century and had been most recently occupied during the War of Independence. Jo walked the grounds of the vast ruins. Ian remained perched on a low stone bridge, his crutches beside him, waiting patiently while she investigated the site.

They headed back to the town center, where they picked up coffee and sandwich wraps and sat outside on a bench, enjoying the weak but warm sunshine.

Jo had been holding off on bringing out her sketchbook but in the colorful town of Kinsale, she couldn't resist. Ian was happy to sit and watch her sketch away. It sure beat sitting in his house, staring at the television all day.

As she set up her kit, she pulled out a wooden box and showed him. "I bought these colored pencils a while ago but have been waiting to use them."

"Why wait?" he asked.

Jo shrugged and smiled. "I don't know. I was saving them for something special." Her gaze bounced around the colorful scenery ahead of her.

They were on a narrow street in the town center of Kinsale. The terraced shops and businesses had been painted in bright shades of purple, orange, pink, blue, and lime green.

"The colors really liven up the place, even in December," Jo observed.

"They do," Ian agreed. Like herself, he thought. It could be the bleakest, darkest day of the year and somehow, he felt she'd brighten up any space she was in. It was just her nature. It wasn't that she was gregarious, but she was kind and genuine, and that counted for something to him.

Jo had her head bent over her sketch pad, drawing in clean strokes. She bit her lip as she studied the object of her sketch and then with a furrowed brow, returned her attention to her pad.

Fascinated, Ian watched her work and marveled at the end result she created on the page.

"You make it look so easy," he remarked.

She lifted her head and smiled at him. "It is, really."

"No, it isn't," he countered with a laugh. "I can assure you, if I attempted to sketch the exact same thing, it would look nothing like that." He pointed to her sketch pad.

Jo laughed. "It was probably the same for you and rugby. I bet people thought the same thing when they watched you play—'he makes it look so easy.'"

"Maybe," he said.

Ian sipped his coffee and looked away. He was pleased to realize he didn't feel angry or bitter when she mentioned his former career. It was like a thought drifting by in a boat. Was this healing? he wondered.

Jo had returned her attention to her work, and Ian was perfectly content to sit there, sipping coffee and watching her draw.

He couldn't remember the last time he'd enjoyed himself so much with a girl.

When they pulled up in front of his house, it was dark. It had been a wonderful day, Ian thought.

As they walked up the footpath, Jo said, "Thanks, Ian, I really had a great time today."

"Me too," he said.

Jo stopped outside of Bridie's.

Ian looked over to his own home and asked, "Did you want to come in for a while?"

Jo sighed. "I would love to, but I should see my Gram. She's going to think I've run away or something."

Ian understood. After a brief pause, he said, "Do you have plans for next week?"

Jo said, "Not really. Loose plans."

"Maybe we could drive over to Kerry or Limerick or even Galway. It's a bit of a hike, but—"

Jo cut him off. "I'd love that."

Ian smiled.

Jo went to the door and waved and smiled at him before disappearing inside.

Oh, Johanna.

Chapter Nineteen

Gram and Bridie insisted on taking Jo dress shopping in town the following morning. The Christmas party was the next day, Sunday.

Jo liked the town. It wasn't as colorful as Kinsale, but it resembled it with the row houses of shops. She was surprised at the number of dress shops in town. There were at least five small shops, each with two windows flanking a central entrance. Most windows featured mannequins dressed in lovely outfits: dresses—or frocks, as Bridie called them—or coats, hats, and scarves.

"Let's go in here," Bridie said, opening a door to one of the shops before Jo or Gram could offer an opinion.

Jo didn't know who was more excited about her accompanying Ian to his Christmas party: Bridie, Gram, or herself. She had to admit to a flurry of nerves as well. She'd never been to a proper Christmas party. She'd only known the day affair for the employees of the shop she'd worked at, but it had always seemed lackluster at best.

But this party, she was excited about. And nervous. She'd been spending a lot of time with Ian, and it had turned out better than she could have anticipated.

Although Gram and Bridie said nothing, Jo suspected they knew something was up. She did not miss their raised eyebrows or their pointed looks. And any time Ian's name was mentioned, they seemed to study her for her reaction.

Ian's grandmother took control of the dress-finding situation, and Jo was glad to let her. Bridie told the saleswoman that Jo needed a frock for a Christmas party.

The woman rested her chin between her thumb and index finger as she contemplated Jo. Finally, she announced, "With your hair color, I'd say something in green. Or even navy."

"Definitely," Bridie said.

"It'll bring out her eyes," Gram said. "They're one of her best features."

Jo laughed. The saleswoman showed Jo to a dressing room and said, "I'll be right back."

While she waited, Jo could hear the two elderly women outside her dressing room, whispering and giggling about someone back in the day named Johnny O'Hare. Jo shook her head and found herself laughing along with them.

When the saleswoman returned with five dresses on her arm, she eyed Jo's bra and underwear. "And maybe some foundation wear?"

Jo's shoulders caved in embarrassment. The bra, though decent enough to hold the girls in proper place, was old. She wore comfortable cotton underwear her grandmother would have been proud of.

"Do you need stockings too?" the woman asked.

"Um, yeah, I didn't bring any. I didn't think there'd be a need," Jo said.

"No worries, I'll get some," the woman said with a smile. "Try those on and see how you get on."

Jo slipped on the first dress, a green print number, but immediately dismissed it because it was too tight in the bust. She quickly stepped out of it and put on the second dress, but she couldn't get it over her hips.

"*Ugh*," she said. She looked at the size and frowned. That was a size too small.

She didn't hold out much hope for the third dress but tried it on. The simple navy wrap dress fit like a glove. Jo studied herself in the mirror and liked how it accentuated her curves.

She stepped out of the dressing room for the opinions of Gram, Bridie, and the saleswoman.

"Oh, Jo," Gram said, "you look beautiful."

"I think we have a winner."

And so it was agreed. That was relatively painless, Jo thought. In addition to the dress, she purchased undergarments and pantyhose. When they walked out of the shop, Bridie said, "Let's go next door and we'll get a pair of shoes."

"Sure, why not?" Jo said. But the visit to the shoe shop turned into an exercise in entertainment as Gram and Bridie got a fit of the giggles, reminiscing about cycling to some dance when they were eighteen.

"And remember that Tomas Gilligan?" Bridie asked with a moue of distaste.

Gram scowled. "He thought he was God's gift to women."

Bridie said to Jo, "He chased us all around the countryside that night on his bike." She shook her head as if the memory was unpleasant.

"What did you do?" Jo asked, curious about this stalker.

"We ditched him!" Gram said, and Bridie erupted in a howl of laughter.

Jo and the saleswoman looked at them, curious.

"We hid our bikes behind a hedge and jumped in the ditch!" Bridie explained.

"It was almost dark. But our frocks and our shoes were covered in mud and muck," Gram said with a grimace.

"But remember he went by on his bike, ringing that stupid bell?" Bridie asked, exasperated.

"And we had to cover our mouths because we were laughing so hard!" Gram recalled.

"He was a right eejit!" Bridie said, shaking her head.

"Whatever happened to him?" Gram asked.

"He ran afoul of a bull," Bridie said, raising her eyebrows. "Wasn't even forty." She made the sign of the cross and added, "May he rest in peace."

"That's a shame," Gram said, crossing one leg over the other and folding her arms across her chest.

"Is it?" Bridie asked, and the two of them started laughing again.

Chapter Twenty

IAN STOOD IN FRONT of his wardrobe, one door wide open, staring at the ties on the tie rack. He sighed. Why had he agreed to go to this thing? Here he was, obsessing over a stupid thing like a tie when what he really needed was his career back.

He'd had some mild anxiety during the day and thought more than once about backing out. But the few times Johanna had mentioned the party, she'd seemed excited about it, and he didn't want to let her down. Then Nana mentioned she'd gone out and bought a dress. He was committed.

As it was the holiday season, he opted for the red tie, throwing it onto the bed with his suit. Glancing at the clock, he knew he had to make some moves. He didn't want to keep his date waiting. At least he didn't have to go far to pick her up.

Did I just refer to her as my date? he thought with a groan. She was a friend, he reminded himself. He paused and sighed. He definitely thought of her as more than a friend. Her lips looked so damn kissable! He wondered if she was only accompanying him to be nice. She probably felt sorry for him. That resulted in a twinge of annoyance. When had a woman ever had to feel sorry for him? Before he could go down that rabbit hole, he showered, shaved, and slapped on some aftershave.

He put on his granddad's cuff links, then rolled his neck and shrugged, getting comfortable in the suit. He took one last look in the mirror before gathering up his crutches and heading down to his Nana's to collect Johanna.

Bridie and Mary were sitting in the front room. In the corner, an Elvis Presley album played on the old turntable. There was a scratchy sound quality to it, and Ian made a note to get his grandmother a YouTube subscription and a Bluetooth speaker.

"Ian, you look so handsome!" Bridie said, jumping up from the sofa.

Mary stood up. "I'll let Jo know you're here."

As Ian waited for Johanna, and his grandmother fussed over him, there was a moment of panic. And a strong urge to remain at home. He wondered if they could just get a takeaway and stay in and watch a movie. Even if he had to suffer through a chick flick.

Johanna appeared in the doorway with her hair all done up, wearing an amazing blue dress and strappy black heels, and all and any thoughts of not going to the Christmas party quickly evaporated.

She was beautiful.

And suddenly, more than anything, he wanted to go to this banquet, and he wanted to go with *her*.

"Hi," she said, smiling. Her red lipstick made her teeth appear whiter. She lifted her hand in a little wave.

"Hi," he replied. He felt a little gobsmacked. Blindsided. He was overwhelmed with the urge to take her into his arms and kiss her properly.

"You clean up well," she said with a smile.

"You look great too!" he said. Boy, was he out of practice. Why hadn't he told her she looked beautiful? Because he didn't want to scare her away. And he couldn't say it now, because he'd waited too long, and it would appear as an afterthought.

There was a momentary pause as they regarded each other. Jo was unusually quiet. But their reticence was countered by the nonstop comments from their grandmothers.

"They make a beautiful couple," Mary enthused.

"Like they were meant to be together," Bridie gushed.

Ian put a stop to this type of talk; he didn't want Johanna embarrassed. "We should get going, Johanna."

"Wait," Bridie said. "Let me get a picture of the two of you in front of the Christmas tree."

"Good idea," Mary said. "They should have a photo as a remembrance."

"Ian, hand me your phone and I'll take a photo," his grandmother instructed.

"Jo, I'll take a photo with your phone as well," Mary said.

They handed over their phones. Ian was not against having a photo of the two of them on his phone. He was only sorry he hadn't thought of it himself.

He laid his crutches on the chair in the corner and hobbled to the front of the tree. He and Jo edged closer in front of his Nana's lit-up Christmas tree. He slid his arm around her waist and pulled her closer. She looked up at him and gave him a smile that felt as if it was just for him. She smelled wonderful, something light and floral. For a minute, it felt as if it were only the two of them in the room.

"I'm excited about this," Jo whispered.

"Are you?" he asked, not quite believing it.

She nodded. "It sounds like it's going to be a proper Christmas party, and I actually have a 'date,'" she said, making air quotes in front of her.

Ian laughed. He began to think that his American counterparts were falling down on the job if she got excited about going to a sports banquet in a foreign country. *She's a strange bird, my Johanna*, he thought with a grin. His grin disappeared as he thought about how he'd just referred to her as "his."

"What's wrong? First, you're smiling, then you actually looked scared for a moment, and now you look distracted." Jo smiled. "What's going on in that head of yours, Ian?"

If you only knew, he thought. "Just some mild anxiety about tonight."

She gave his hand a reassuring squeeze. "Me too!" She wore a cheeky grin and added, "Who'd think to look at us that we'd have the same problem?"

He laughed. "Johanna, I can assure you, you have nothing to be anxious about tonight."

She beamed, her whole face lighting up.

Ian felt like the luckiest guy in the world.

"All right, smile!" Bridie instructed.

Ian and Jo smiled broadly as their grandmothers took their picture.

Chapter Twenty-One

All Jo could think about on the drive to the hotel where the Christmas banquet was being held was that not only did Ian smell good, but he looked so handsome. She almost suggested that he should wear a suit and tie more often. She had worn her coat, as the air was damp, but at least the rain had stopped. She was wearing her hair in a complicated updo with a lot of hairspray. It wouldn't be a good idea to stand near an open flame. Bridie had made an appointment for her that afternoon at the hair salon in town to get her hair and makeup done. She rarely wore her hair up, and she usually wore minimal makeup to work, so it was fun to get all dressed up for a change.

Jo stole a glance at Ian in the passenger seat. He'd been quiet on the drive, and she wondered if he was having second thoughts. She hoped not. This would be good for him. Gradually, he was getting out of the house, and she bit her lip as she hoped that after she returned to the US, he wouldn't retreat back into his shell. That once she'd gone home, he'd continue moving on.

As much as she tried not to think about returning home, it hovered there, always nearby. She wasn't looking forward to leaving Ian, and she wondered how they would leave it. She could hardly entertain the thought of a long-distance relationship, as they hadn't even kissed or talked about anything like that. It would certainly make for a great vacation romance. She could only hope, but she was unsure as to how Ian felt. And she wasn't quite brave enough to ask him what would happen next.

"Why are you so quiet?" Ian asked, his voice disturbing the silence.

"I was wondering the same thing about you," Jo asked.

"Just thinking," he said.

"About anything in particular?" she asked.

"Wondering if this is a good idea," he said. He turned his head to stare out the window.

"It'll be fun," she said. "You have food and Christmas music, so what's not to like?"

Although this garnered a laugh from him, he did not respond.

After a few minutes, she said, "Ian, we don't have to stay all night. There's no rule book here saying we have to stay until the bitter end."

Ian nodded. "All right."

"But promise me you'll try to hang on until after we eat dinner."

Ian burst out laughing. "Where do you put it, Johanna? It's all you talk about. Eating."

"I know. I have a speedy metabolism. I'm always hungry."

"It sounds more like a false appetite," he mused with a smile.

At least he was smiling, she thought.

It was a start.

After dinner, Jo excused herself to go to the ladies' room. She'd cleared off her plate. The food had been fabulous. Roast beef with Yorkshire pudding. Creamy mashed potatoes. Roasted vegetables. For dessert, there was Victoria sponge with ice cream. When Ian pushed his dessert plate over toward her, she looked at him and asked, "Are you sure?"

"I am. I insist." He laughed.

"Well, if you insist," she said.

As she headed out of the dining room toward the restroom, she glanced back at him, but he was surrounded by former teammates and in the midst of conversation. She was glad. It had turned out to be a good night so far. People had been coming up to him continuously, and it appeared that he had been truly missed. They were sitting with Donal and Brian and their girlfriends. Both girls were friendly, and Jo didn't feel like the outsider she was.

She couldn't remember the last time she had felt this happy. Here she was in Ireland at Christmas, and she'd met a guy she was truly interested in. In two days, her parents and her brother would be flying in for the holiday, and she couldn't wait for them to meet Ian.

The new year was just around the corner and unlike other years, this one held so much promise.

It was all good.

Chapter Twenty-Two

WHILE IN THE MIDST of conversation with his former teammates, all trying to convince him to return to the team in some capacity, Ian kept one eye on the entrance to the dining room for Jo, waiting for her return.

When she finally appeared, he relaxed. He caught her eye and she broke into a wide smile. Heads turned as she made her way back to their table. Ian wondered if she had any idea how pretty she was.

Jo arrived at the table. "Did I miss anything?"

"Not a thing."

When she was in her seat, Ian leaned toward her and whispered, "You are a very pretty woman, Johanna."

Pink tinged her cheeks and neck, and she reached for her water glass and took a sip. It was as he thought. She had no idea. And she wasn't used to hearing it. In the future, he planned to remedy that.

He studied her for a moment, although he didn't have to. The way she looked tonight had been seared on his memory. The gorgeous auburn hair swept up like a crown around her head. The way the dress accentuated her curves and her shapely legs.

When she didn't say anything, Ian said. "You know, it works both ways."

"What? You want me to tell you you're pretty too?" Jo teased.

Ian burst out laughing. "No, what I meant to say is we don't have to stay the whole night. We can leave whenever you want," he said, referring to their earlier conversation, giving her a way out.

She laughed. "Okay."

"We could go somewhere else," he said, hopeful. He wanted to be alone with her.

"Could we?" she asked.

He smiled. "It's early. Not even ten."

She nodded. "If you want. I'm ready whenever you are."

"Are you sure? Do you want to ask the kitchen for another plate of food before we take off?" he teased with a grin. "Maybe they could pack you a light lunch or something, to tide you over until we reach our next destination."

She threw her head back and laughed. He loved when she did that. To be in her orbit when she laughed like that, it made him feel like it was just the two of them, even in a crowd of people.

Ian gave Jo directions to drive toward the city. He glanced at her in the driver's seat. She was managing the gears all right; there'd been no grinding. It was nothing short of miraculous.

"So, did you enjoy yourself?" Ian asked. He certainly had but was glad to be alone with her.

"I had a ball," she said.

"You didn't mind that we couldn't dance?" he asked.

"Not at all."

Ian shook his head. Johanna was so refreshing. She was different from any other girl he'd been with. He wondered what sky she fell from.

"Where are we going now?" she asked.

Ian chuckled. Always game for the next thing. Always a good sport. So open-minded about seeing new places. He didn't know what he was going to do when she went back to the States in January. He chose not to think about that in this moment. For tonight, he was out with a pretty girl who made him laugh, and he was going to enjoy himself.

"I know exactly where we're going. Turn left here," he said.

She made the left, and that brought them onto the main avenue of the city.

"Look at all the lights!" she enthused.

For as far as the eye could see, magnificent Christmas lights—some clear, others colored—crisscrossed overhead from one side of the street to the other.

"It's not that cold. I thought we could go for a stroll and take in the lights." He winced. The thought had sounded good but when he said it aloud, it had come out sounding corny and lame.

"I'd love that!" she gushed.

Maybe it wasn't so corny after all.

"Let's see if we can find a parking spot on the street." After four blocks, he pointed to an empty space and Jo pulled in. That was the easy part. It took six or seven tries for her to straighten the car out against the curb.

"There we are," she said, smiling.

Ian shook his head.

Once they got out of the car, Ian glanced at her footwear and her coat, which wasn't much. His eyes lingered on her legs for a moment. They were mighty fine.

"Johanna, if you get cold or your feet start to bother you, let me know and we'll go home," Ian said. He himself was impervious to cold. He just had to be mindful of the crutches on the pavement.

Jo walked by his side. Silently, he cursed the crutches. He would have liked to hold her hand.

His Nana used to bring him to the city at Christmastime as a young boy. At the end of it, there'd be a stop at some restaurant for tea and a sweet. He chuckled at the memory of it.

"What's so funny?" Jo asked.

He smiled. "Just thinking of when Nana used to bring me down here to look at all the lights and decorations."

"My Gram and I used to do a lot of baking at Christmas. She used to let me help," Jo said thoughtfully. "Though I suspect I was more of a hindrance than a help." She crossed her arms against her chest.

"Are you getting cold?" Ian asked.

She shook her head. "Not at all."

All the shops were closed, but their windows were done up in decorations and lights. They stopped at each one, looking at it in wonder.

"I hope someday to bring my children down here at Christmastime," Ian said out loud. He wished he hadn't said that.

"Would you like to have children someday?" Jo asked softly. She stood next to him, but they both focused their attention on the window display of life-size carolers, fake snow, and a Victorian lamppost.

"Sure, it's what life is all about," he said quietly. "What about you?"

"I would. Someday."

He could picture her as a mother. She was so kind and sweet; her kids would be lucky to have her. An image flashed in his mind of the two of them together in the future with little children around them. His eyes widened at the thought of it.

After a few moments of silence where the future seemed to hang in front of them, Ian suggested they move on.

There were some restaurants and pubs along the way. From some of the rowdier establishments, the noise spilled outside onto the pavement, but Jo and Ian kept moving.

Ian slowed to a halt and leaned on his crutches in front of one particular basement pub. Jo stood next to him. He stood at the railing and stared down the stairs. They could hear the music from the interior. Not Christmas music, but traditional Irish music with fiddles and accordions. From inside came the sound of boisterous music and patrons clapping.

"I used to come here all the time." Ian looked at the stairs again and sighed. He remembered them as being steep and treacherous even when he wasn't on crutches. Had he two good legs, he would have taken Johanna by the hand and led her down to the pub.

"Do you want to go in?" Jo asked.

"Sure, I want to go in, but I can't get down the stairs." He tried to keep the frustration out of his voice. He didn't want to ruin what so far had been a perfect night.

"Maybe—"

Ian was already shaking his head. Whatever her idea was on how to get him down the stairs, it wouldn't be one he would approve of. Of that much he was sure.

Before he could reply, three couples approached, each linking arms. They began to amble down the staircase. But the first guy stopped, noticed Ian, and said, "Hey, aren't you Ian Twomey from the Irish Rovers? Are you going in, mate?"

Realizing that all eyes were on him, Ian's skin prickled. "Nah, another time."

But the guy in the leather jacket was heading back up the stairs to Ian. "Come on, Tom, we got this. Bobby, grab his crutches."

Ian was about to protest when Jo laid her hand on his arm and gave him a beseeching look.

The two men got on either side of him, and he wrapped his arms around their shoulders and used them as support to get down the staircase. At least they hadn't offered to carry him. Even he still had a little bit of pride left. The staircase was a bit narrow, so it was tight on the way down.

The guy named Tom quipped, "One of us is going to have to go on a diet."

Even Ian had to laugh.

At the bottom, they set him down, and the one named Bobby handed him his crutches.

"Thanks," Ian said.

"Don't mention it. It's the least we can do after all the entertainment you gave us on the field," the first guy said. "I'm Rory, by the way. We're here for the night most likely, but when you're ready to leave just let us know."

"Thanks again," Ian said.

Ian followed Jo up to the bar and got the barman's attention. He ordered a pint for himself and a Coke for Jo. He also asked the barman to send a round of drinks over to the three couples.

From the bar, they looked around for a seat. A couple stood up from a table at the wall, and the man waved them over. Jo carried the drinks and followed Ian.

"We're just leaving," the man said.

"Thanks." Ian let Jo slide into the booth first, and he set his crutches against the wall before sliding in next to her. When they were situated, he glanced up to see the other couples lifting their drinks up to him and nodding in acknowledgment. He returned the gesture.

The pub was dark and small and narrow. But it was packed. An old-timer hunched over his ale at the bar, an untouched pack of cigarettes next to his pint glass. Two older men tended the bar, and Ian had been coming in here long enough to know that they were brothers and had owned the place for decades. The rumor was that the two brothers hadn't been on speaking terms for over twenty years and every once in a while, they'd take their fight outside, settle it with some swinging fists, and return to their pub to pull pints.

A group of musicians was seated on stools on the other side of the room: two fiddle players, someone playing the concertina, and a man who played spoons on his thigh.

Ian leaned back and draped his arm along the length of the booth behind Jo's head. The night had turned out better than he had expected.

It was after one in the morning by the time they left, and another half hour before they were home, chatting and laughing all the way. As they pulled up in front of the house, Ian said, "You know, Johanna, I had a great time tonight. Thank you so much for going with me."

"I had a wonderful time. And the food!" she enthused.

Ian let out a bark of laughter. It always came back to the food with her. They sat in the car in front of the house for a few minutes, and finally, aware of her hitched breath and her chest rising and falling, and emboldened by the success of the night, he turned to her and leaned in to kiss her good-night. She met him halfway. He closed his eyes and his lips found hers. She tasted good, like mints and something sweet. He kissed her gently, then more insistently. She curled her fingers around the lapels of his jacket and pulled him closer to her. He reached his arm around her back.

When they pulled apart, each leaned back in their seats. Jo had a dreamy expression on her face.

"Thank you, Johanna," he said.

"No, thank you!"

He laughed and he continued, "No, but seriously, thank you for helping me to feel normal again."

"You are normal," she protested.

He smiled. She was so good.

"Anyway, your family is coming in on Tuesday, so don't worry about me, I'll be fine. Spend time with them. You can even use my car if needed."

"Thanks. Dad has rented a car, so we're all set."

As they got out and parted ways on the footpath, Ian said to her, "I'll see you in a few days."

Surely, he could wait, couldn't he?

CHAPTER TWENTY-THREE

As Jo climbed into bed, exhausted but happy, her grandmother rolled over in her bed on the other side of the room.

"Did you have a good time?"

"I had a wonderful time," Jo replied. She'd felt like Cinderella at the ball.

"I'm so delighted to hear that," Mary said.

"But Gram, I feel bad," Jo said, all of a sudden overcome with guilt.

Mary turned toward her and in soft shadow from the nightlight, a frown appeared on her face. "Why do you feel bad?"

"I've hardly seen you since we arrived. I thought we would go sightseeing around Ireland, but you and I have hardly spent any time together," Jo said. She'd been so enthralled with Ian that she'd mostly left her Gram to her own devices. What kind of granddaughter was she?

"Pay no mind to that." Mary laughed.

"But wouldn't you like to do something together?" Jo asked.

Her grandmother seemed to be struggling. "Jo, as much as I would like to do things with you, more than anything, I want to spend time with Bridie." Her voice caught. "We're both in our eighties now, and we've known each other since we were four. The distance never interrupted our friendship. We talk every Sunday, and when I see her, we pick up right where we left off."

"You're lucky, Gram."

"I know I am. And I know when I leave Ireland this time, I will not be coming back," Mary said softly. "We don't say it, but Bridie and I both know that after this trip, we will probably never see each other again."

Jo swallowed hard, trying to get words out around the lump in her throat.

Neither said anything for a moment until Mary said in a drowsy voice, "This is your trip as much as mine. It makes me happy to see you enjoying yourself so much. I hope someday you love Ireland the way I do."

She was beginning to drift off, and Jo whispered into the semi-darkness, "I think I already do."

CHAPTER TWENTY-FOUR

IAN HADN'T SEEN Jo since the night of the Christmas party. He had hung back; she was busy with her family, driving her father's rental car. From Nana, he'd heard they had gone to Killarney and Kenmare.

The truth was, he missed Jo. Things weren't the same without her there. Things seemed bleak and desolate. But he'd kept busy. He did some Christmas shopping online for his parents, Nana, and his sisters. He was appalled at the rush delivery fee, but he'd no one to blame but himself for leaving it until the last moment. On the morning of Christmas Eve, he made a phone call to Frank, the physical therapist, to set up an appointment in the new year. It was time to start moving on. He'd even surprised his parents by ringing them to see how they were doing. It only took his mother a moment to recover from her surprise over hearing from him before she launched into how she'd received the photo of him and Jo going to the Christmas party. Ian grinned. His grandmother was a little savvier with technology than she let on.

He spent a lot of time thinking of moving on with Jo. He had no clue as to how they would manage a long-distance relationship but if she was agreeable, he'd figure out a way. He was already thinking about when she could return to Ireland or when he could possibly visit the States.

Jo's family squeezed into Bridie's sitting room on Christmas Eve.

Bridie and Mary ran back and forth to the kitchen, serving cake, tart, and tea and refusing any offers of help from Jo or her family.

Ian thought Jo's family was nice. Her parents and her brother, Marc, all seemed genuine, friendly, and easy to talk to. Ian had expected nothing less; after all, the acorns usually didn't fall too far from the tree. At least that's what Nana always said.

Once everyone had a plate of dessert and a cup of tea, Bridie and Mary returned from the kitchen and sat down with the group, setting their plates in their laps. Ian thought both women looked tired. They'd been on the go every day since Mary and Jo had arrived. And there had been plenty of late nights. Ian didn't know how they did it. They had a lot of years behind them. But he also knew that when Mary went home in two weeks, Nana would be lonesome without her.

And Scruff had taken a shine to Jo's mother and was currently resting on Mrs. Mueller's lap. Barbara Mueller petted the dog as she talked.

Jo sat across from him on the sofa, ensconced between her parents. She looked really pretty tonight. Her hair hung in loose waves, and she wore a green blouse and black skirt. Ian had a hard time keeping his eyes off of her. The rest of them were dressed in casual wear, and the grandmothers had decided on ugly Christmas jumpers, which did not disappoint. But Johanna—she stood out like the star on top of the Christmas tree.

"It all worked out well in the end, didn't it?" Mr. Mueller said to no one in particular. To his mother he said, "You got to see Bridie, and at Christmas too, so that makes it extra special." He took a belt of his tea, and there was a rumbling of agreement among them.

He turned toward his daughter. "And you, worrying about money and how you were going to earn your keep," Bill continued with a laugh. He bent his head, cutting a bite of tart with his fork.

Jo gave her father a quick smile and stared at her hands in her lap.

"More tea, Bill?" Bridie asked, jumping up.

"No, thanks, I'm fine, Bridie," Bill said. He looked at Ian. "Well, Ian, how was our girl?"

Ian blinked, uncomprehending. "I'm sorry?"

"Does she get a good performance review?"

Ian wasn't sure what Mr. Mueller was rattling on about. What had he thought his daughter was doing with him? He didn't think he wanted to know. Jo had her head bent, not looking at him or anyone, for that matter. He cast a quick glance over at his grandmother and noted that she had gone pale.

Ian frowned. "I'm not sure I'm following you, Mr. Mueller."

Bill gave a dismissive wave, and Ian wondered briefly if he'd had too much Irish whiskey.

"I'm talking about Jo being your paid companion," Bill explained.

Ian stared at him. His gaze bounced over to Jo, who had finally lifted her head. Her cheeks were stained red. His eyes landed on his grandmother, who was concentrating on the Christmas cake on her plate as if she had never seen one before. She added nothing, which made Ian immediately suspicious.

"What did you say?" he asked. He wanted to make sure he understood correctly. Jo, a paid companion?

Bill Mueller was only too happy to fill in the blanks. "Jo was so worried about coming to Ireland at Christmastime. She needs to work to pay her rent, you know."

"No need to go into all that, Bill," his mother said to him with a pointed look.

Bill carried on, oblivious. "What a stroke of luck for Jo to work here while she's on vacation. Bridie came up with the idea. And it all worked out. You got out of the house, and Jo got to see Ireland and got paid for it."

"I think Jo should go into nursing," Marc chimed in.

Ian saw red. He could feel the muscle in his jaw twitching. He looked from Nana to Mary, and then his eyes landed on Jo. No one met his gaze. They'd all conspired behind his back. And was he such a desperate case that they had to *pay* someone to keep him company? He looked back at his grandmother. All that talk about doing her a favor. *Show Jo around, keep her company because she'll be bored hanging around the two grandmothers.* That hadn't figured into it at all. Here he was, thinking he was going out of his way to keep Jo company, showing her Ireland, spending just about every waking minute with her, and that had nothing to do with it.

His gaze bounced back to Jo and stayed there. He'd thought there was something between them. That they had a connection. Granted, it had only been a short time, but he really *liked* her. He liked her to the point where he was trying to figure out a way to continue the relationship after she went back home.

Ian gritted his teeth. She'd been playing him. It was like a punch to the gut. He had her all wrong. She came across as all sweetness and light, but she was a conniver and a chancer and a rogue.

The walls of the sitting room seemed to be closing in on him. The room felt hot. A fine sheen of perspiration broke out on his forehead. His stomach flipped. All he knew was that he had to get out of there.

He leaned forward and set his empty plate on the coffee table.

"Well, that's it for me," he announced. "I've got to go home."

Nana's head snapped up. "You can't go home now! It's Christmas Eve and it's too early."

"I've got a headache," he said, picking up his crutches, which were leaning against the armchair. He was upright and now heading toward the door.

"Here, let me get that for you, young man," Bill said, hopping up from his seat and opening the sitting-room door for Ian.

"Thanks," Ian said. He added over his shoulder, "Enjoy your stay in Ireland."

"Ian!" Nana called out, following him out and shutting the sitting-room door behind her.

Ian stopped at the front entrance, leaning on his crutches.

"It's not how it sounds," she started.

"Really? Because it sounds like you paid Johanna to keep me company." Only the fact that she was his grandmother and elderly prevented him from lashing out.

"It was just to give her some pin money while she's here," Nana explained.

"How much were you paying her?" he asked.

When she told him the amount, he blanched. "That's an awful lot of pin money."

His grandmother's eyes were shining and darting about. "But look, it doesn't matter because after a few days, she refused the money anyway. Ian, she never took a dime."

"How gallant," he said through gritted teeth.

She laid her hand on his arm. "This isn't Jo's fault. It's mine."

"Why didn't you tell me?" he demanded. "Why lie to me?"

"Because you would never have agreed to it," she said firmly. Her resolve, which had wavered, was returning in full force. "Think about it. If I had told you that Jo was going to be your paid companion, you would have said no."

Ian sighed, knowing what she was saying was true. It still didn't give them the right to lie to him.

"And you have to admit that you and Jo have hit it off. You've been having a good time," his grandmother said.

Ian leveled his gaze at her. "That's over now. I don't ever want to see Johanna Mueller again."

She laughed nervously. "Ian, you can't be serious—"

Ian's gaze was steely, and Nana stopped talking. "I don't want anything to do with her. It may have turned into something, but the beginning of our relationship was built on a lie."

Nana stood there, her mouth agape. Ian slipped out the door and closed it behind him.

It was dark and there was a light mist falling. His anger propelled him up the short footpath between his house and his Nana's. He'd just reached his front door with the lighted wreath when he heard footsteps behind him. He turned and saw Jo approaching him.

"Ian," she started.

Ignoring her, Ian unlocked his door and it swung open.

"Ian, please—"

"Don't, Johanna."

"Let me explain," she pleaded.

He turned on her. "What is there to explain? I have all the information I need. You were hired by my grandmother to keep me company. And all this time, I thought I was doing you the favor. I feel like the biggest fool in Ireland."

He stepped over the threshold.

"I am sorry," she said. "Can I come in?"

"Are you serious?" he asked. When she didn't answer, he continued. "No, you can't come in. In fact, I don't ever want to see you again."

Jo flinched at his words, but Ian didn't care. "All this time, I've been thinking we got along great these past few weeks. I really enjoyed your company and thought it was the same for you."

"Ian, I didn't take any money from your grandmother," she said in a pleading voice.

"When did you decide that? Before or after I kissed you?"

Jo looked as if she'd been slapped. Her eyes were wet and her chin quivered. "I am so sorry," she whispered.

"Apology not accepted," he said, closing the door on her.

CHAPTER TWENTY-FIVE

Jo's cheeks were on fire as she made her way back to Bridie's. Through the front window, she could see her family and Bridie sitting around, talking. The Christmas tree sparkled brightly. When she arrived back at Bridie's front door, she realized she wasn't up for a crowd, even if they were family. Even if it was Christmas Eve.

She pulled her winter coat tighter around her and headed further down the footpath until it joined the main one that led through town center. She needed to walk and clear her head and most of all, she needed to be alone.

What had she done? And more importantly, how could she make Ian understand that it had never been a job for her? That her feelings for him were genuine.

She headed toward the main section of town. It was quiet. Everything was closed and there was no traffic. Everyone was home, celebrating the holiday with their families.

As she walked, she was oblivious to all the decorations and houses with lit Christmas trees in their windows or front halls, or exterior lights strung up all over the place.

In her life, she'd never seen anyone so angry with her as Ian had been. She had known this was a bad idea, and now everything was ruined. But what was worse was that he totally questioned her reason for being with him. She liked how she felt in his presence. She wanted to be near him. To hear the sound of his voice or smell his aftershave. Or to sometimes catch the way he looked at her when he thought she wasn't looking. She wiped away the tears.

After a brisk walk, she decided that she would leave it for now. It was probably best to leave him alone and let him cool down. They weren't leaving yet; there was still time to talk about this and clear things up. Surely, he would see sense. Wouldn't he?

As Jo climbed into bed, Gram sat across from her, rubbing lotion onto her hands. Gram looked tired, and Jo suspected the last few weeks were starting to catch up with her. It didn't seem to slow her down though.

"Are you all right, Jo?" Gram said, keeping her eyes on her granddaughter.

Jo shrugged and sat on the side of her bed, kicking her slippers off. "I feel awful about what happened. He's so *angry*."

"I suppose Ian Twomey has a lot of anger in him right now due to his situation," Gram said. "Him finding out about you being paid—well, that has tapped a nerve. I bet if it had happened before the accident, he wouldn't have been so angry."

Jo didn't want to point out that if it were before the accident, Ian wouldn't have needed a companion and most likely wouldn't have wanted for female companionship, especially of the leggy blonde variety.

She waited for Gram to get into bed before she turned off the light.

Gram yawned and within minutes, was snoring lightly.

Jo lay awake for a long time in the dark, tears stinging the backs of her eyes. The trip had been wonderful. Until it wasn't.

She didn't know how to fix things between her and Ian. She hoped she could before she left on the seventh of January. There was plenty of time to make things right.

On New Year's Eve, it was pouring. Rain slammed against the roof. This time of year, the sun set early. By five, it was as black as pitch outside. And dawn didn't arrive until almost eight thirty in the morning.

Jo had not seen Ian since Christmas Eve. Her plan to let him cool down and then talk to him flew out the window when Ian surprised everyone by purchasing a last-minute ticket to Spain to spend Christmas with his parents. He'd called Bridie from the airport, informing her that he'd bought a one-way ticket and wasn't sure when he'd be home.

Luckily, Jo had been too busy to dwell on it and fall into a pit of despair. Christmas Day had passed in a blur. The day after Christmas, she went with her parents and brother to spend a few days over in Galway. They spent a few nights there, and their days were busy with bus tours. They'd just arrived back in time for New Year's. Then tomorrow, they were off to Dublin for three days before her parents and her brother flew back to the US. She followed her parents and brother all over Ireland. But her sketch pad remained undisturbed in her backpack. She had no interest in that. The only plus side was getting to spend some time with her brother. Back home, he was so busy with med school it seemed they never had time to sit and talk. So, she was grateful for that. It proved to be a wonderful distraction from her sadness.

As soon as she landed at Bridie's, she asked her, "Have you heard from Ian?"

Bridie shook her head. "I'm sorry, Jo, for everything."

Jo nodded. "Maybe he needs some time, and the sunshine certainly would help." She tried to be optimistic, feigning a lightness she didn't feel.

"That's it," Bridie said, but she looked unconvinced.

Well before midnight, Jo said good night to everyone.

"You're going to bed? But it's New Year's Eve! Don't you want to ring in the new year?" her father asked.

"I've got a headache, so I'll see you in the morning."

"I hope you're not coming down with anything," her mother said, a frown etching her forehead.

"No, it's only a tension headache. We've been so busy these last few days," Jo said with a forced laugh.

"And we've been having a great time," her father added.

"We have, Dad," Jo said.

In her room, she pulled out her sketch pad and neatly tore a piece of paper off the seam. She'd write a letter to Ian and slip it under his door before she left.

"In the past, this day, January sixth, was known as the Women's Christmas. It was a day reserved just for women," Bridie told Jo as they drove to the hotel for a meal. "On that day, the women were free from their chores and the men waited on them."

Gram snorted in the front seat next to Bridie. "Although as the years went on, it became simpler to go out for a meal. My own father—may the Lord have mercy on him—he could deliver a calf with his eyes closed, but cook a meal?" Gram laughed. "Never. My mother usually went to her sister's house for the day."

"Bridie, what did you used to do for Women's Christmas?" Jo asked.

"My Jim tried to cook a dinner the first year we were married. At the time, I thought it was quite progressive of him," Bridie said. She erupted in giggles. "But it was disastrous. His roast was as tough as shoe leather, and his apple tart . . . My goodness, I couldn't tell you what went wrong there. I've never seen a tart so soupy."

"But it was nice that he tried," Jo said.

"It was marvelous! Because of that, it was probably my favorite Women's Christmas. He tried so hard!"

The hotel was packed. Jo noticed it was all women. The dining room was all done up in gold-and-white Christmas decorations. The walls were painted a pale aqua with white trim. All the tables were covered in white linen tablecloths and adorned with red and white flower arrangements. She joined Bridie and Gram at a table near the window. The day was bright, which helped to lift her mood.

The meal consisted of three courses, and Jo chose a black pudding starter, roasted lamb for dinner, and a flan with fresh berries for dessert.

Jo couldn't help but wonder what Ian was doing in Spain. She wondered if they celebrated Women's Christmas over there. Sorrow filled her at the thought that they were leaving the next day and she hadn't had a chance to see him one more time, to clear things up. It felt unfinished. And just plain awful.

Her head snapped up. "I'm sorry, Bridie, did you say something?"

"I asked how your flan is."

"Oh, it's lovely," Jo said.

Gram and Bridie talked about the wonderful time they'd had. Jo was happy for her grandmother. It truly had been the trip of a lifetime for her, and it was good that she got to see Bridie again.

"You know, Bridie, I just had a thought," Gram said. "I think you should come over to me next year for Christmas."

"You know, Mary, I just might!" Bridie said.

CHAPTER TWENTY-SIX

I AN READ THROUGH JO's letter again. In the eleven months since she'd left, he'd read it so many times that the paper was now soft and worn.

Dear Ian,

I was hoping that we could clear things up between us before I left. I'm sorry to have missed you.

For as long as I live, I will always regret not being upfront with you from the beginning. It has cost me much. I understand that maybe you don't feel the same way about me that I feel about you, due to all that has happened without your knowledge. It is understandable.

Things happen. Sometimes, there is no reason for it. People are involved in accidents and sustain life-changing injuries. Family members do stupid things to help the ones they love because they can't bear their suffering. And foolish girls fall in love with guys they have no business falling in love with.

I realize that we will probably never see each other again. And I realize that you probably don't even want a friendship, and I will try to accept that. But I do hope that someday, you will be able to forgive me.

—Johanna

There really was no need to read through it again as by this time, he had it memorized. This one piece of paper made him feel connected to Jo, no matter how tenuous that connection was. He sighed. Over the last eleven months, he really should have responded or gotten in touch with her. But he hadn't. What would he say? How could they pick up where they'd left off? They had parted on bad terms, and that was on him. But he had an idea, so all was not lost.

Carefully, he folded up the letter and slipped it into his pocket. He headed up to his Nana's house. It was nice not to have to use the crutches anymore. After months of physical therapy, he had almost full range of motion with his ankle. But he could always tell when the rain was coming by the way it ached. Christmas was only weeks away, and he couldn't believe another year had come and gone. But he was in a much better place than he had been a year ago.

Nana was in the spare room with a suitcase open on the bed. She went through piles of clothes, and some she placed inside the suitcase, others she left on the other twin bed.

"Oh, Ian, there you are." She smiled. "Would you like some breakfast?"

Ian shook his head. "No, Nana, I'm fine. Are you almost ready for your trip?"

Her eyes sparkled. "I am! I can't wait to stay with Mary, and she has all these things planned for us. Bill and Barbara are taking us to New York City to see the sights. Rockefeller Center at Christmastime! It's like a dream come true."

Ian fingered the letter in his pocket, trying to strengthen his resolve. "I was wondering if you'd like some company on your trip."

Nana paused, holding a folded nightgown in her hands. "What do you mean?"

"I was thinking of going with you," he said quietly. "I want to see Johanna."

Nana burst into a smile. "That's wonderful. Of course you can come with me. They'll be so delighted!"

Ian held up his hand. "You can tell Mary, but I'd like to surprise Johanna." It was going to be a surprise all right. Since the last day he'd seen her, he had done nothing but think of her. Constantly. All the time. He needed to say some things to her, and he didn't want her to know he was coming in case she refused to see him.

"That'll be wonderful. I always had high hopes for the two of you," Bridie said. She set her nightgown in the suitcase.

"Did you plan that too? You and Mary? The matchmaking?" he asked.

Nana grinned. "No, but I wish I had thought of it. My only concern at the time was getting you out of your house and out of your rut."

Ian nodded.

"What about work?" Bridie asked, going back to her sorting and packing.

"I took some time off," he explained. The previous February, as he was contemplating taking a position with his team, Sky Sports had contacted him about a commentator/analyst position for the televised games. He'd jumped at the chance. It involved a lot of travel, but he found he was a natural for the position. He loved it.

"Will I take Scruff out for you?" he asked.

"That would be a help. The poor thing doesn't know what's going on. He saw the suitcase come in from the garage and he bolted," Nana said, shaking her head.

Ian paused in the doorway. "Nana, about all that—last year—thanks for looking out for me."

Nana smiled and walked over to him and hugged him. She barely came up to his chest and felt tiny when he wrapped his arms around her.

"That's what nanas are for," she said. "To have your back."

He kissed the top of her head. "Thanks."

"Now go on, this suitcase won't pack itself," she chided.

He called the dog, and Scruff scrabbled across the tile floor to the front door, where Ian hooked the lead onto his collar. Christmas couldn't come fast enough. The thought of seeing Johanna buoyed him. He stopped in his tracks as a thought hit him. What if Jo had moved on? What if she had a boyfriend? Was he so arrogant he thought he could swan in and sweep her off her feet? He was starting to have second thoughts.

For the next three blocks as he walked the dog, he bolstered his resolve with the thought that he'd just hop on a plane and come back home if she wasn't receptive to him. Either way, he was going to say what he needed to say and then move on with his life, either with her or without her.

Over the past year, his ears always perked up any time Nana mentioned she'd spoken to Jo's grandmother. At first, he'd asked if there was any news on Jo, and then it got to the point where he didn't need to ask her anymore. She just told him.

Jo had been busy since she'd left Ireland. Through the grandmothers' grapevine, he'd learned that she had given up her apartment and moved back in with her parents. She'd started with some classes at the community college last semester and had enrolled in a degree program at the university near her parents' home back in August. Her news was all good, and Ian was happy for her. There'd been no mention of a boyfriend or dating, and he hoped that was the case.

Once Scruff had been walked, Ian took his grandmother to town for some last-minute shopping before the trip. He'd traded in his old car for a newer model, and it had been good to be driving again.

After their trip to town, Nana talked him into going to the mall, where he finished his Christmas shopping.

Once they were home, he went to his own house to pack his suitcase, anxious to get to the States to see Johanna.

Chapter Twenty-Seven

S NOW FELL AS Jo made her way across the college quad. Her last exam for the semester was over, and she could now enjoy her Christmas vacation. She wouldn't be returning until the third week in January.

As she hurried across the campus, someone yelled out, "Merry Christmas, Jo!" Without stopping, she turned and waved. It was that guy from her art class. He was friendly, but Jo liked him right there: in the friend zone.

The parking lot shone with ice, and Jo treaded carefully until she reached her car. While the engine warmed up, she brushed off the snow. Before she headed home, she was going to stop at Gram's. Bridie was in town, and Jo was eager to see her. Gram had given Jo her recipe for mince pies, and Jo had made a couple of practice batches in her mother's kitchen, to which her father had given two thumbs up.

She threw the snow brush into the back seat, buckled herself in, and carefully eased the car out of her parking spot.

Gram was so excited about Bridie coming over for Christmas that she was like a child who still believed in Santa Claus.

Although Jo was looking forward to seeing Bridie, she also wanted to hear the news about Ian. From what her grandmother had told her over the course of the year, it seemed as if Ian was doing great. A new job as a sports analyst, traveling, success with the physical therapy, and Gram had told her that he was "in a good place." Jo was delighted for him, but she couldn't help but wonder if he ever thought about her. Thought about her the way she'd thought about him. There had never been mention of a girlfriend, but that didn't necessarily mean there wasn't one. Gram might have withheld that kind of information to spare her feelings. She was determined to get the answer from Bridie.

As she pulled onto Gram's street, Jo decided that maybe it was time to move on instead of continuing to pine away hopelessly. After all, her own life was falling into place. She'd given up the apartment, moved back home, and was going to college for an art therapy degree. She was excited about her prospects. She'd been at her barista job at the coffee shop for almost a year. The owners—a couple with young children—were wonderful to work for. Because they baked fresh every day, employees were allowed to take home the leftovers at the end of the day. What a perk! So much different from her last job.

Jo parked her car in Gram's driveway. She went around to the back porch. When she opened the door, she was greeted by a blast of heat, the muted sound of Christmas music, and the smell of cinnamon. Laughter floated out from the living room, and Jo smiled to herself. Apparently, Gram and Bridie had picked up right where they'd left off.

In the kitchen, she removed her hat and scarf and laid them on the back of a chair. Once her coat was removed, she fluffed her hair with her fingers and headed toward the living room.

"Bridie!" Jo exclaimed when she saw her seated next to Gram on the sofa. But she pulled up short when she spotted Ian getting up from his chair opposite them.

A rush of joy filled her. "Ian? What are you doing here?" Her heart was thumping so fast she could feel it in her throat and was afraid the sound might drown out his answer.

Everyone stood up.

"Hello, Johanna."

Before Ian could explain his presence, Jo found herself wrapped in a hug from Bridie. Jo squeezed her back gently, happy to see her.

"Jo, look at you! Your hair is so long! It's beautiful," Bridie said.

"Thank you. It's so good to see you, Bridie," Jo answered.

Gram said, "Bridie, why don't we go into the kitchen and make some tea? I've got some eclairs, and Jo's been busy making mince pies."

"Sounds wonderful!"

They were gone, leaving Jo alone with Ian.

Jo turned and focused her attention on him. He stood there with his hands in his pockets. She thought he looked well; he stood straight and tall without the crutches, and she was glad to see he was still sporting a beard and mustache.

"You look great, Johanna," he said.

"Thank you," she said. Confusion filled her. She hadn't heard from him in almost a year. Hurriedly, she added, "You look well too."

"You're probably wondering what I'm doing here," he started, shuffling his feet.

"I am curious," she said. They remained apart. She was unsure if she should hug him; he might not welcome that.

"I wanted to see you," he said.

"Really?" she asked.

"Really." He smiled.

"Why?" She folded her arms across her chest.

From inside his breast pocket, he pulled out an envelope and withdrew a sheet of paper. Jo recognized it immediately. She pressed her lips together.

"I wanted to ask you about this," he said.

Jo didn't say anything. She couldn't. She was frozen to the spot. He'd saved her letter? What could it mean? She didn't want to get her hopes up. Not again. She couldn't do that again.

"What did you want to ask?" she ventured.

"Did you mean what you said?"

Jo's shoulders sagged. "I meant every word of it."

"Even the part about foolish girls falling in love with guys they had no business falling in love with?" he said quietly.

Oh, that part. Jo felt her cheeks go hot. "At the time, yes, I did," Jo said bravely, even though her voice shook.

"And did you? Did you fall in love with me?"

She nodded, not taking her eyes off him. She held her breath.

"Johanna, I'm sorry for how things ended between us. I was not in a good place, but that doesn't let me off the hook. You didn't deserve that."

Jo gave a weak smile and shrugged. She wasn't sure what she was supposed to say. She also noticed that it had gone awfully quiet in the kitchen.

Ian took a step closer to her.

He closed his eyes and sighed before opening them. "See, the thing is, I was falling in love with you too. It was hard not to."

Jo's eyes widened. "Then what was the problem?"

"At that time, I was in no position to offer you anything. Truthfully, I was angrier at myself than you, but I projected it onto you. I hope you can forgive me."

"Of course," she said. "But I didn't want anything from you. I only wanted you."

"At that particular time in my life, I didn't even have that to offer you."

Jo bit her lip, waiting, expectant.

"But I've spent the last year getting back on track, getting my life in order." Ian glanced down at the floor. "And I'll understand if I'm too late. It'll be my own fault, but I was wondering if you would have me. I mean, if you would give us a try. See where it goes."

Jo had to restrain herself from jumping into his arms. Her enthusiasm was tempered by reality and distance. "Ian, we live so far away from each other. How would this work?"

"I know it would be difficult, but I'm willing to do whatever it takes. In between broadcasts, I'd come over to see you, and I was hoping you'd come to Ireland on your breaks," he said. "There's email and Skype to hold us over."

Jo smiled. He'd given this some thought. That warmed her, the thought that he'd been thinking about their future. And how they could make it work.

Ian shifted nervously on his feet. "What do you say? Will we give it a go?"

Jo leaped into his arms. "Yes!"

Ian grinned, breaking into laughter. "That's my girl." He set her down and pulled her tightly into an embrace, kissing her.

From the kitchen came the excited whoops of their grandmothers.

Epilogue

January 6th, 5 Years Later . . .

"Stop peeking, Johanna!" Ian mock scolded, chasing her out of the kitchen.

"I just wanted to know if you needed any help," she said with the lift of an eyebrow.

Ian put his hands on his hips. "I don't need any help. I'm managing."

With a grin, Jo nodded toward his apron. It was hers, actually, and it had red ties and was covered in apples. "The apron suits you!"

She took a step back, laughing, but he caught her by the wrist and pulled her to him, kissing her. "Listen, Mrs. Twomey, how am I going to put this dinner on for the Women's Christmas if you keep harassing me?"

Jo shrugged, giggling, and leaned in to kiss him again. "It smells good. What is it?"

Ian pulled away. "Oh no you don't. You're not going to trick me into ruining the surprise."

"I'm surprised already," she said.

"I know I'm not known for my cooking—"

"That's because you've never done it," Jo pointed out.

A timer went off behind them in the kitchen, and Ian looked toward it and then back at her.

"Did you want me to get that?" she asked.

He shook his head. "No, I'll get it. Maybe you can collect Nana? It's almost ready."

"Sure," she said. Reluctantly, she pulled away from Ian, grabbed her coat, and bounced out of the house.

As she made her way to Nana's house, she smiled to herself. She was happy. They were just back from the States, where they'd spent Christmas with her family. Marc had been there with his wife, Stacy, and their new baby, Lindsay. Gram, like Nana, was now ninety, and she'd finally moved in with Jo's father and mother. The last time she and Bridie were together was last spring, when Jo and Ian had gotten married.

They decided to live in Ireland, mainly because of Ian's job. Jo had found work with the Health Service Executive, Ireland's public health service provider, as an art therapist. Her time off was spent driving around Ireland with Ian, sketching ruins, people, donkeys, and landscapes.

She knocked on the door and stepped into Nana's house.

"Nana?" she called out.

Nana appeared with her coat on, a bit frailer looking and slightly stooped over. She'd slowed down considerably since she'd fallen and broken her hip two years previous. But she was still formidable. Now she had a carer and home help coming out to the house daily.

"Should I eat a sandwich before I go there?" she asked with a twinkle in her eye.

Jo laughed. "No, I think it'll be okay. It smells good, whatever he's cooking. And he's picked up a cake from Dash's bakery in town," Jo said.

"We can always fill up on cake if the dinner is a bust," Nana said. "Hopefully, he'll do better than his grandfather."

"I think it'll be fine."

Nana nodded and linked her arm through Jo's as they walked back up to their house.

Nana had her eyes glued to the footpath, watching where she was walking. "You know, he must really love you if he's going to all this trouble to cook a meal for you on the Women's Christmas."

"He wouldn't even let me do a load of wash this morning. Took the basket right out of my hands," Jo said.

Nana stopped walking. "He's got it bad then."

Jo laughed. "We both do."

NOTE

To stay up to date with new releases and receive exclusive bonus material, sign up for my newsletter at www.michelebrouder.com

ALSO BY MICHELE BROUDER

Coming in 2026

The Gallagher Brothers of Galway Bay
Fake Dating, Irish Style

Escape to Ireland
A Match Made in Ireland
Her Fake Irish Husband
Her Irish Inheritance
A Match for the Matchmaker
Home, Sweet Irish Home
An Irish Christmas

Happy Holidays
A Whyte Christmas
This Christmas
A Wish for Christmas
One Kiss for Christmas

A Wedding for Christmas

Hideaway Bay
Coming Home to Hideaway Bay
Meet Me at Sunrise
Moonlight and Promises
When We Were Young
One Last Thing Before I Go
The Chocolatier of Hideaway Bay
Now and Forever

The Lavender Bay Chronicles
The Inn at Lavender Bay
Lost and Found in Lavender Bay
Second Chances in Lavender Bay
New Beginnings in Lavender Bay
Looking Back in Lavender Bay
Sisters and Friends in Lavender Bay

Soul Saver Series
Claire Daly: Reluctant Soul Saver
Claire Daly: Marked for Collection

All romance and women's fiction titles are available in ebook, paperback, and large print paperback. Audiobooks are currently being rolled out.